It's an
AARDVARK-EAT-TURTLE WORLD

Also by Paula Danziger:

The Cat Ate My Gymsuit
The Pistachio Prescription
Can You Sue Your Parents for Malpractice?
There's a Bat in Bunk Five
The Divorce Express

It's an AARDVARK-EAT-TURTLE WORLD

Paula Danziger

Delacorte Press/New York

Published by
Delacorte Press
1 Dag Hammarskjold Plaza
New York, N.Y. 10017

Copyright © 1985 by Paula Danziger

Library of Congress Cataloging in Publication Data

Danziger, Paula [date of birth]
It's an aardvark-eat-turtle world.

Summary: At fourteen, Rosie, her mother, her best
friend, and her best friend's father form a new
family unit and find it takes a lot of work to make a
family in a world of changing relationships.
[1. Divorce—Fiction.   2. Family Life—Fiction]
I. Title.
PZ7.D2394It   1985   [Fic]
ISBN 0-385-29371-2
Library of Congress Catalog Card Number: 84-17645

Manufactured in the United States of America

First printing

TO THE MENSCHES—Jane and Happy Traum
and THE MENSCHLINGS—Merry, Adam
and April (who said, "I'll believe it when I see it.")

ACKNOWLEDGMENTS AND THANKS TO
THE WRITING CONNECTION —Annie Flanders,
June Foley,
Patricia Reilly
Giff, Francine
Pascal
THE ARIZONA CONNECTION —Sandra, Charles,
and Susan
Nelson
THE METUCHEN CONNECTION—Jackie Owen, Bill
Contardi
THE CANADA CONNECTION —Jerry and Leona
Trainer, Hy,
Judy, Tema, and
Jojo Sarick, Barb
Issett

It's an

AARDVARK-
EAT-TURTLE
WORLD

1

If a Prince Charming or a Prince Semi-Charming came up to my door and said, "Rosie Wilson, you are the most beautiful, individualistic fourteen-year-old in the universe," I certainly wouldn't slam the door in his face.

There's something even more important to me than that, though. What I really want more than anything is to be part of a family, all living happily under one roof.

My parents divorced soon after I was born, a fact that I have tried not to take personally.

I used to beg my mother for a baby brother or sister.

She'd say, "Bite your tongue."

For a long time, I thought that was how babies were made.

By the time I found out how babies were really born, I had permanent tooth marks on my tongue.

My mother—Mindy—and I get along really well, which is good because we live together in Woodstock, New York.

Until recently I used to ride a bus that is nicknamed the Divorce Express. Almost every weekend I would go down to Greenwich Village, this really great area of New York City, to see my father. Then he and his second wife and her two kids moved to California. Actually, I was glad that his wife and her two kids went. I'm just sorry that my father left with them.

So it's not as if I'm an orphan or anything. I do have a family . . . just not one that's living all together, in the same place.

It's all changing now. I'm finally going to get my wish. In one week I'll be part of a family. My mother and my best friend's father have fallen in love and are going to live together. Mindy and Jim. Phoebe. Me.

Once before, Mindy and I lived with someone, Andy. It didn't work out for them, for us.

This time I hope it does.

I want this to start out with ". . . and they lived happily ever after" and get even better.

2

The Donners' dog just ate the pet of the month, and I've called Phoebe to come right over.

The Donners are the people I baby-sit for. They have one three-year-old kid, Donny, whom Phoebe and I refer to privately as the Little Nerdlet.

They also have a dog, Aardvark. Aardvark is the one who just ate the pet of the month.

The Donners joined this club that sends some little pet to kids each month. Last month it was a goldfish. It died in two days. The Little Nerdlet and I held a burial at sea, actually down the toilet.

So today the new pet arrived. I took the package out of the mailbox and brought it inside.

The Little Nerdlet had to go to the bathroom. I went with him. He likes company while he's sitting there.

Aardvark got the package off the table, and by the time I came back the paper was shredded all over.

From the torn feeding instructions and the little pieces of shell, it seems obvious that the pet of the month was once a turtle.

As I wait for Phoebe to arrive at the Donner house, I think of something my father always says about life: "Rosie, it's a dog-eat-dog world."

In Phoebe's and my lives, I guess, it's an aardvark-eat-turtle world.

3

By the time Phoebe gets to the Donner house, everything is under semicontrol.

The pieces of the turtle are in a Crayola box awaiting burial.

Aardvark is hiding out somewhere under the porch.

The Little Nerdlet is eating a chocolate-covered yogurt pop and talking to Phoebe about turtle heaven.

I'm feeling a little worn out.

"I think we must bury the turtle," the Little Nerdlet says. He has chocolate all over his face.

"I think we can wait." I try to clean him up.

"No." The Little Nerdlet backs away from

me. "Don't take it off. I want to be the same color you are."

I look at him and then at Phoebe.

We both start to laugh.

"It's not funny." The Little Nerdlet starts to cry. "I want to be the same color Rosie is."

I pick him up, hugging and kissing him. "Donny. I'm this color because my father's black and my mother's white. You can't be this color. You're white."

"You're brown. Not black. Not white." He puts more chocolate on his face. "So now I'm brown too."

"He's got a point." Phoebe smiles.

He puts a grubby hand on her face. "Now Phoebe is our color too."

Phoebe doesn't even take the gunk off her face, although she's usually really careful about looking good. In fact, she puts even more gunk on.

"The turtle went to heaven," the Little Nerdlet informs me as I put him down.

I decide not to get into it with the kid. With a white Jewish mother and a black Protestant father, I try to stay out of religious discussions.

I wonder what the turtle was. Protestant. Jewish. Catholic. Muslim. Hindu. Maybe Unitarian.

He probably was shy and didn't come out of his shell easily.

Maybe he was a she.

Thinking about these earth-shattering questions is too overwhelming, so I decide it's time to bury the turtle.

We take the Crayola box outside and put the deceased into the ground.

I look at Phoebe and her chocolate-yogurt-smeared face and am glad that we've been best friends since we met last year, when she moved to Woodstock full-time.

I look at the turtle grave and wonder whether it was excited about going to its new house.

If what happened to the turtle is an omen about what it'll be like going to our new house, I'm going to be shell-shocked.

4

"Whose bright idea was it to move both of our households into our new home on the same day?" Jim, Phoebe's father, asks. He sits down on a rolled-up carpet.

"Yours," Phoebe says. "It was definitely not my idea."

"Three hair driers. Four clock radios. Sixteen boxes of books. Two sets of silverware. Assorted dishes and glasses. Three stereos. Hundreds of albums and tapes." He puts his head in his hands. "And we've only just begun to unpack.

"It seemed like such a good idea at the time." He shakes his head. "This way no one feels like he or she was here first. We all start out equal, together, one family."

"One tired family." I pretend to faint.

Mindy goes over to Jim and gives him a neck and shoulder massage.

I start to unpack another box because I don't want to look.

I wish they wouldn't touch each other in front of me.

Mindy says, "Maybe we should have a garage sale or put some of this stuff into storage and take it out if the other breaks or wears out."

"I think we should hold on to everything for a while, just in case this doesn't work out and we have to split up." The words are out of my mouth before I can stop them.

There's silence for a few minutes—a very loud silence.

"I'm sorry." I bite my fingernail. "I never should have said that."

It means so much to me that we're a real family. I even had to give up my cat, Fig Newton, and my dog, Salamander, because Jim's allergic. That's how much I care.

Finally Jim says, "On our first night together as a family, let's not talk about breaking up already. I want us to be a family."

He looks hurt.

I want to cry. "Jim, I want this to work out, more than anything. I just get scared sometimes that the things I really want won't last."

Jim comes over and hugs me. "Honey, I know that it's hard to be certain of any relationships.

But I really want this to work and will do my best."

"Me too." Mindy looks determined.

"I'm willing to try," Phoebe says.

"I've got an idea. Let's make up our own ceremony to commemorate the beginning of our lives together." Jim claps his hands.

He just loves to turn events into special occasions.

We all look at him, waiting for elaboration.

"We've done enough work for tonight. Why don't we all go back to the old house, take a swim, and have the ceremony there." He jumps up.

"Jim, there's so much to do," Mindy says. "Don't you think we should be practical?"

He sits down again.

Mindy starts to laugh. "I don't believe that I just said that we should be practical. That sounded like something my mother would have said. Unpacking all of these boxes must have temporarily deranged me."

"Actually it's been a very moving experience for me," I tell everyone.

They all groan, and then Jim says, "Okay, let's all go over to the pool."

"I don't know where my swimsuit is." I stare at the mess around us.

"We could always go skinny dipping," Jim kids.

My mother smiles and nods.

"NO!" Phoebe and I both yell at the same time.

Sometimes parents can be so embarrassing.

"Let's all just go over there in what we're wearing and jump into the pool that way." Jim's not going to give up on his idea.

We all decide to go for it.

Just before we leave, Mindy says, "Listen, everyone. If we're really going to have the ceremony, let's have it here . . . not at the other place where there are old memories. This is the time for us to make new memories."

I understand. The place where Phoebe and her father used to live was the place that her parents bought before their divorce. Her father got it in the settlement and her mother got the New York City apartment.

Jim puts his arm around Mindy and kisses her.

I tie my shoelace so I don't have to watch.

"Honey, I'm sorry. Would you rather we didn't go to the other house at all?" he asks.

She kisses him back.

I tie my other shoelace.

I hope they don't kiss again. I've run out of feet.

Mindy says, "It's hot tonight. It's the last time we can use the pool before the new tenants move in. Of course I want to go swimming. I'd just like to have the ceremony here, not there."

"Okay, then let's all hold hands right this very instant." Jim grabs Mindy's hand, then Phoebe's, then mine. Our hands are all mashed together. It's a good thing that he's got such big hands so we all fit.

"This is so sudden," I say. "It's like we're eloping. I've always wanted a big formal wedding."

"For your own, your very own, you can do that. For this one, we'll be much less formal." Jim grins.

What an understatement. He and Mindy are wearing cut-off jeans. He's got one of his political T-shirts on, the one that says A WOMAN'S PLACE IS IN THE HOUSE . . . AND IN THE SENATE. That was a present from Mindy. His ex-wife used to give him shirts with alligators on them.

Mindy's got her long blond hair piled up on top of her head. She's wearing one of Jim's shirts that he uses when he's oil painting.

I'm wearing one of my favorite outfits—a thrift-store Hawaiian shirt, an old pair of gym shorts, and a beaded headband.

Phoebe's wearing sweatpants and a T-shirt that used to belong to her boyfriend, Dave.

We're definitely not going to make the cover of *Bride* with our outfits.

"We should all say something. I'll start." Jim looks a little nervous. "I just want everyone to know that I love you all very much . . . all in special ways, separately. And I love us together and will do my best to honor our commitment to be a family."

Mindy nods. "Me too. And we'll all work to-gether to honor the originality and creativity in each of us."

That makes sense. With Mindy trying to write a children's book and Jim trying to earn a living as an artist, that's a very important part of our lives.

Phoebe kind of clears her throat and doesn't say anything for a minute. Finally she says, "I just want to be the best daughter that I can be . . . and the best sister to my best friend."

I can feel my tears starting. I feel like a real nerd until I look around and see that I'm not the only one crying. "I want us to live with love . . . and understanding . . . and I don't know what else to say. Isn't there supposed to be some-one else here to say 'I now pronounce you man and wife' . . . or husband and woman . . . or man and woman . . . and kids . . . or some-thing like that?"

No one is quite sure of what comes next.

Then Mindy says, "Jim. Mindy. Phoebe. Ro-sie. Listed alphabetically—equally. We are now pronounced a family."

We all hug and kiss.

It flashes into my head that some people might think this whole thing is kind of weird.

But I don't care.
The old way didn't work.
Maybe this one will.
I certainly hope so.

5

The room looks like a cyclone hit it. We got back too late from swimming to try to get it together.

Normally, I'm a very neat person. Since I was about four years old, I've been straightening up after Mindy, who believes in "creative disorder."

Actually the room looks like it was hit by two twisters—dueling cyclones.

The walls and ceiling are the only areas not cluttered by clothes or boxes.

We have, however, already hung up our favorite posters, so the walls are not spotless.

Phoebe's put up one of my least favorite posters—the one with the upside-down possum with its tail attached to a tree limb. It says "Hang in there." She's also hung up one of my favorites, the Sierra Club picture of a beautiful forest. My father, who loves baseball and is always making up statistics for life, would probably say that Phoebe's batting .500 in P.O.W. (Posters on Wall).

On my side of the room, I've put up what Mindy calls "an antique poster." There's a flower on it and the saying "War is not healthy for children and other living things." Next to the poster I've put up a picture of my father, taken when he was playing in a jazz concert in New York City.

Phoebe's still asleep. She's one of those people who like to wake up at around noon and stay up all night. I, however, am a morning person, up and cheerful at practically the crack of dawn.

The phone rings.

It's not anywhere in sight.

Leaning over, I look under my bed for the phone. It doesn't seem to be there. Leaning farther forward, I lose my balance, do a flip, and fall out of my bed.

My gym teacher would give the manuever an A+, except that as I fell my foot hit Phoebe's bed. Also her hand, which is hanging off the bed.

The phone stops ringing.

I'm lying in a pile of clothes, wondering whether a search party is going to have to be sent out to find me in the clutter.

Phoebe's eyes open. She leans over. "Are you okay?"

"Sure." I get up, making sure that nothing's damaged.

Phoebe stretches. "I heard the phone and then I felt your foot hit me. Have you invented a new alarm clock?"

I check under her bed for the phone. "It was a once-in-a-lifetime experience, not a new family ritual."

"Thank goodness," Phoebe says. "Listen, do you think that was Dave calling me?"

She crawls out of bed. "Where's the phone?" She looks in the closet.

I point to her corner of the room. "Look under that pile of clothes."

The Snoopy phone is under a down vest.

Dropping the vest back on the floor, Phoebe asks, "Think it's too early to call Dave? His father has a fit if I call too early on weekends."

"Wait," I say, although I really have no idea of what the rules are. Phoebe's the expert in the dating department. "If that was Dave, he'll try again."

Phoebe steps over her clothes. "Rosie, I have a BIG favor to ask."

The last time she had a BIG favor for me was when we had to pull eighteen frogs and two kamikaze mice out of her swimming pool.

I wait to hear what it is.

"Now don't say yes unless you really want to do it," she says.

I continue to wait.

"It's just that I had trouble going to sleep last night," she says. "I think it was because my bed is so close to the window. Would you mind if we moved our beds around? Be honest. It'll be okay if you don't want to change. I can get used to it."

I laugh. "I was just trying to be nice letting you have the place where you can look out at the universe. That's where I really wanted to be."

She smiles. "And I was trying to be nice and let you have the snugly closed-in part of the room."

We talk about trading beds, try each other's out, and decide to keep our own.

As we move our beds around, Phoebe says, "What if neither of us had said anything and then in fifty years we finally discussed it and found out that we'd always hated where our beds are? I'm glad I mentioned it."

We change our posters around.

Then Phoebe flops back into bed.

I begin to unpack my boxes. Out of them come some clothes, my old sticker collection, and treasures found at flea markets: two beaded bags, a stained-glass jewelry box, an old copy of *Bound for Glory*, by Woody Guthrie—a real early folk singer whose music I love. I also unpack the books that my grandmother on my father's side gave me. *Roots*. Books by Toni Morrison, Alice

Walker, James Baldwin, Sharon Bell Mathis, Rosa Guy, and John Steptoe. Poetry by Countee Cullen and Langston Hughes. Lots of other novels. My grandmother told me never to lose track of the black part of my heritage, not that I ever would.

Phoebe says, "I'm going to call Dave now."

The phone rings like magic, as if Dave knew to call.

Phoebe picks up the phone, listens for a minute, and then crosses her eyes and puts a finger to her head as if it were a gun.

It's obviously not magic, at least not the kind that Phoebe wanted.

It's got to be her mother from that reaction. That's sort of like going to pull a rabbit out of a hat and coming up with slug slime.

All the kids we hang around with call things we don't like slug slime. That's because there was an invasion of them this summer—these disgusting, fat, snotlike creatures, oozing their way through gardens.

Anyway, it's Slug Slime City for Phoebe when she has to deal with her mother.

I try not to listen, but it's hard not to.

Phoebe's pretending to pull a knife out of her heart.

It's a good thing the phone doesn't have a TV screen attached.

Phoebe's shaking her head. "Aw, Mom. Do I really have to go to Canada with you and

Duane? Can't I stay in Woodstock? . . . It'll be the last week before school starts. . . . I know I promised, but it's going to be so BORing there, not knowing anyone."

Phoebe pretends to hang herself with the telephone cord. "I know they have kids, but what if I don't like them? . . . What if they don't like me?"

She sighs. "I know—I didn't have to ride the Divorce Express every weekend because I promised to spend this time with you to make up for it. But we're just getting settled here and I want to stay."

Phoebe looks at me, crosses her eyes again, and acts as if she's gagging herself.

I pretend to hold up a barf bag.

Finally Phoebe sighs and says, "Okay, Mom. I know I'm whining. I give in. I'll go. What kind of clothes should I bring . . . or should we just plan to shop there?"

Sometimes I think that Phoebe is in training for the Olympics marathon in shopping . . . and that her mother is her coach. It's lucky her mother and stepfather have so much money. I once gave her a button that says "Born to Shop."

Phoebe hangs up the phone. "Five days with my mother and Duane the Drip, Plastic Pop, the Slug Slime Stepfather."

I say, "Look at the bright side. Canada should be a great experience. I'd love to go someplace new."

Phoebe shrugs.

The phone rings.

This time it is Dave.

They make plans to go to Opus 40 to hear the concert.

Phoebe's always had boyfriends. Moving here, she almost immediately started going with Dave. I, who have lived here for years, am going to Opus 40 with the Little Nerdlet.

I go out to use the bathroom, the only one in the house. There's already someone in it. As I cross my legs, I think about the place where Jim and Phoebe used to live. It had two bathrooms in the house and one in the pool cabana, and that was just for the two of them.

Now there are four people living in a house with only one bathroom.

Maybe we should assign each person certain days when they have to limit their liquid intake.

It would have been so nice to live in the other place, except Jim's getting a lot of rent money and he needs it now that he's trying to make it as a full-time artist.

Mindy also felt that it was important to start life in the new place together and also not have the bedrooms too close to each other.

"Too close," hah. I know what that means— too close for Mindy and Jim to have sex in their room if it's right next to Phoebe's and mine.

I don't see why they couldn't just cool it. Make out quietly or something. Anyway, they're getting old. Sex shouldn't be so important to middle-aged people.

I knock on the bathroom door. "Whoever's in there, please hurry up. I've got to get in."

The door opens. Mindy's there in a bathrobe, with a towel wrapped around her head. Jim is also in there with a large bath towel wrapped around his body.

They act as if there is nothing unusual about the situation. As they walk out, each of them kisses me on the forehead.

I rush into the bathroom, saying nothing.

I'm not sure why I get so weird when I think about Jim and Mindy "doing it."

When I was much younger, I used to ask my mother about all sorts of things that confused me. If I really couldn't understand something even after she explained it, she would tell me to put it in a file called "Life's Little Mysteries—to be solved, maybe, at a later time."

I guess that the whole question about why I'm so weird in this situation belongs in that file. I'd put it right under the one about "If five pounds of feathers were dropped on your head from the top of the Empire State Building, would it feel any different from five pounds of steel?"

I've never understood that one either.

6

After leaving the bathroom, I stand in the hall of our new house, getting used to it.

There's still the smell of fresh paint, but underneath that is the sort of musty wonderful aroma that most old Woodstock houses have.

In the background I can hear the wind chimes that Mindy put on the porch.

I feel good in this house, I think as I reenter the bedroom.

Phoebe sees me and starts jumping up and down. "I've got something to tell you."

I guess. "You've hired Professional Maid and Maintenance to clean up our room."

"No, better than that," she says. "This is great news. My mother's invited you to go to Canada with us. Remember how you said it would be fun to go? I called Mom back and told her how much happier I'd be if you came along. She said we'd take you as an early Christmas present."

"But it's August and anyway, why should they give me a present?" I sit down on the bed.

"An early present for me." She sits down on my bed. "Please come, Rosie. I'll be your best friend."

"You already are," I tell her.

She smiles. "I'll be your best best best best friend."

I grin.

She begs some more.

I think about it.

The Little Nerdlet's family will be away on vacation so I won't miss work.

I was just planning to hang out with my friends, which would have been great, since I've spent so much time baby-sitting.

Canada—my first foreign country . . . airplanes, which I love . . . new people . . . it sounds exciting.

"Yes." I clap my hands. "I'd love to go."

Phoebe claps her hands too. "We're going to Canada."

"I hope that Mindy says yes." I pick up a pair of shorts and fold it.

"Of course she will," Phoebe says. "Are you kidding? It'll give her a chance to be alone with my father."

Phoebe doesn't sound as if she's overjoyed by the prospect.

"Let's go find them." Phoebe grabs my hand and pulls me out of the room.

We find Jim and Mindy in the living room, fully dressed and hanging pictures.

They love the idea.

I can tell by the way they're smiling at each other that Phoebe was right.

"What about spending money?" Mindy asks.

"I can use some of my baby-sitting money," I offer.

Mindy nods. "Great."

Phoebe and I jump up and down and hug each other.

Then we hug Mindy.

Then we hug Jim.

The doorbell rings.

It's Dave, Phoebe's boyfriend.

He joins in the hugging.

With everyone hugging, there's one point where Phoebe and Dave are together and so are Mindy and Jim.

I start to unpack another box and wonder what's keeping Prince Charming. Here I am, fourteen years old, and there's no romance in sight.

Is it because I'm part black?

Is it because I'm part white?

Is it because I'm part ugly?

Perhaps the Prince has lost the directions to

my new house and doesn't know where to find me.

Jim puts everyone back to work. "Let's get some of these pictures on the wall."

Phoebe and Dave look at each other, like they'd rather be doing something else—like going somewhere private in his car to make out. She says that they do that a lot.

"To work," Jim says.

They smile and help with the pictures.

We put the one that used to be at Mindy's and my house, NEW YORK IS BOOK COUNTRY, next to the photograph of the four of us at the Ulster County Fair.

As we hang one of Jim's landscape paintings, the doorbell rings again.

It's Mr. Donner, the Little Nerdlet's father. He's come to pick me up.

As I leave, I look at our new house and then at the mailbox. Jim's been at work. There are three names on it. Brooks (Phoebe and Jim), Kovacs (Mindy), and Wilson (me). And a rainbow's painted on the mailbox.

I guess that makes it official.

We're home.

7

The Little Nerdlet's pretending to be a gorilla.

It's enough to make me go ape.

"Chee. Chee." Making weird noises, he scratches his head.

"Shh. Your mommy's trying to sleep."

Mrs. Donner's expecting Little Nerdlet Number Two, so she takes a lot of naps. Actually, I think she just wants to escape when the Little Nerdlet gets hyper.

He jumps up and down, yelling "Banana, banana."

I give it to him. The kid really has appeal. (I'd tell Donny that, but I think he's a little young for puns.)

At noon Mr. and Mrs. Donner get it together,

packing the car with blankets, folding chairs, toys, and us.

We get into the car and head to town.

Mr. Donner calls out, "Tourist time. Let's count the number of out-of-state license plates."

Woodstock's very busy. People are going in and out of shops. Some kids who study mime are dressed as clowns and are pretending to be robots.

It's a typical Woodstock near-the-end-of-summer day.

As Mr. Donner stops the car, Mrs. Donner says, "Rosie and I will shop. The two men can wait in the car."

The Little Nerdlet is crying as we leave.

Mr. Donner makes faces to try to distract him.

Mrs. Donner puts her arm around my shoulders. "Rosie, I just figured that you need a little rest. You're so good with Donny. We all think you're so special."

I stumble over my feet, say thanks, and change the subject.

We go into the food place, Bazaar, and pick up some great food for a picnic.

Back at the car the Little Nerdlet greets me as if I'd been gone for years.

To get to Opus 40 we leave Woodstock and go to Saugerties, the next town over. What a weird name for a place—saw-grr-tease. It sounds like a report about a mischievous wild animal.

Driving down a dirt road and parking the car, we see all sorts of other people arriving.

There are people of all ages, since there are going to be a whole lot of different kinds of bands and groups playing.

The Little Nerdlet lets go of my hand and drops to the ground, pretending to be a slug.

I pick him up before he decides to ooze.

As we walk along, I see a lot of the kids from school whom I haven't seen all summer. The kids that I like but don't see out of school.

I also see some of the gang of kids that I do spend time with.

Milton Meyers, who only answers to his nickname, Garbage Gut, and to announcements that food is being served, comes up to me. He proposes. He's been doing that since second grade, when he fell in love with the lunches that Mindy used to make for me. It's kind of a tradition. He proposes. I refuse.

The Donners and I sit down in the middle of this wonderful place, Opus 40. I love it. Some guy, Harvey Fite, bought this old stone quarry and started making stone sculptures and formations. His plan was to work on it for forty years, but he fell off his tractor and died during the thirty-seventh year. So it's not finished, but it's still incredible.

It's in the middle of the woods with mountains all around. There's a fountain, with water flowing down. There's sculpture in different places on the grass.

The colors and textures are really incredible. The cold gray of the stone, the green mountains and grass, the trees, the sky and clouds, the fabrics and colors of people's clothes. It's overwhelming.

I notice that Mindy and Jim have arrived and are sitting down with friends. They look like they've always been a couple, as if they've been together forever, like the rock at Opus 40.

As the sun starts to go down, the place begins to look different . . . a quieter kind of beautiful and peaceful.

The concert begins. The Woodstock Mountains Revue starts it. They play really great folk music. It's not the kind of music that you see or hear on MTV, but I love it. What's also so fun is that lots of other musicians and singers come up onto the rocks and join them. Since it's a concert for nuclear disarmament, there are a lot of people performing. That's another one of the special things about living in Woodstock. There are a lot of fantastic music people living in the area or visiting friends.

Next there's a band that plays rock and roll and more modern stuff. People are dancing along with the music.

During the intermission Mr. Donner takes Donny to the men's room while I rush to the women's room. Time for a break. I want to get

there before the line's too long and I have to
spend the whole time waiting.

It's okay. The line's short and moving quickly.

On the way back I stop at the table where food
is being sold. There's also a souvenir T-shirt of
today's concert on sale. It would be great to have
but it's not really in my budget.

Phoebe comes up next to me. "Let's buy one
together."

I debate for a split second. "Sure."

We buy stuff and share it a lot. We did that
even before we knew we were going to live together.

As we make the purchase, I hear Mindy say,
"Hi, kids."

We turn around.

She seems a little nervous. "The guys are busy
playing Frisbee. I thought I'd come over and talk
to Phoebe for a few minutes alone."

I stick my nose up in the air and say, "Okay.
I'll leave and go eat worms somewhere."

Phoebe puts her hand on my arm and says,
"No. Don't be silly. I want you to stay."

The three of us go over to a place where no
one else is standing.

"Phoebe," Mindy begins. "I hope you don't
mind my mentioning this, but I don't think it's a
very good idea for you and Dave to park in front
of the house and make out like you two did this
afternoon."

I guess the whole day was not spent hanging pictures.

Phoebe backs off.

I stare at Mindy.

This really doesn't sound like her.

She continues. "I'm sure you can see my point."

"That's my business," Phoebe snarls at her.

Mindy shakes her head. "It's everyone's business if you're making out in front of the neighbors and everyone."

Phoebe stares her down. "What an obnoxious thing to say. How can you tell me what's right when you and my father live together and aren't even married?"

Mindy says, "Phoebe, you're overreacting."

"Who do you think you are to tell me what I should and shouldn't do? You're not my mother." Phoebe stamps her foot.

"I was just trying to be helpful." Mindy glares at her.

"Help like yours I can do without." Phoebe looks furious.

Jim comes up to us. "How are three of my favorite people doing?"

"Not good," Phoebe informs him.

"Not well." He always corrects our grammar without even thinking about it.

"I've had it." Phoebe backs off.

"What's going on?" Jim wants to know.

"Ask her." Phoebe gestures toward Mindy.

"She's your friend. She'll tell you what to think about what's going on."

Phoebe turns and walks away.

I knew it was too good to last, feeling good and happy about being a family.

Maybe that's really the way it is.

All I know is that a little while ago I felt great and now I feel absolutely miserable.

Something tells me that Phoebe's feeling the same way.

And Jim.

And Mindy.

8

Phoebe refuses to talk to Mindy.

Jim tried to reason with Phoebe but she wouldn't listen, so now they're not talking to each other.

That leaves Jim and Mindy talking to each other and to me.

Mindy is absolutely furious with Phoebe and feels that she's trying to sabotage the new arrangement.

Phoebe talks to me.

I'm the only person talking to everyone.

Whatever happened to our family vows? Why is it that the one thing I want most in the world is turning to slug slime?

Phoebe sits on her bed, brushing her hair.

"You've got to admit it, Rosie. Your mother's wrong, really wrong."

I start to untangle some jewelry that's gotten jumbled in the move and don't answer.

"Come on," Phoebe persists. "Mindy had no right to say what she did, to butt in like that. Admit it. You wouldn't like it."

I shake my head. "It isn't like Mindy to make judgments like that . . . to butt in. Of course, I've never made out in a car in the front yard, so this is a new experience for her. Maybe it just freaked her out."

Phoebe brushes her hair harder. "Mindy's wrong, and it's not fair that Dad's taking her side. Don't you start taking her side too. . . . Why couldn't things have stayed the way they were? With us as best friends but without them falling in love."

She says "falling in love" as if it were a plague.

I sit quietly, intent on separating my long beaded earrings from a Mickey Mouse pin.

Phoebe stops talking.

Part of me wants to tell her to cool off, that Mindy was wrong but so was she. The other part doesn't want Phoebe to be angry at me too. There's enough fighting already.

Phoebe says, "Rosie, talk to me about this. Come on, you're my best friend and we've always been able to tell each other everything. I don't want to stop just because of HER."

I look up. "HER. You mean Mindy, my

mother, the person you've always liked and confided in. That's the HER you're referring to, right?"

"Past tense . . . used to like," Phoebe says. "Quit siding with her. She's not perfect."

"I never said she was," I say. "But she cares a lot about you and you know it."

Phoebe makes a face.

"Well, it's true." I think about what I should do, what I really want to say, and decide that I've got to speak my mind. "I think you're being impossible not talking to them and making everything disgusting to spoil our new family."

"Blame me." Phoebe raises her voice. "That's it, all my fault. Your mother, the beautiful little saint, had nothing to do with it."

"My mother's not a saint, but she's a good person. She's always been nice to you. You're not giving her a chance."

"Traitor—with a best friend like you, I don't need enemies. You just try to be so good and have everyone like you. You drive me nuts."

That's it. I've had enough. "You don't want a best friend. You want a best mirror, someone who reflects you." I get up to leave the room.

As I reach the door, I turn around and say, "You don't care about this family. You just care about yourself. When you're ready to be and have a real friend, talk to me then. Until then, I don't want to have anything to do with you."

Before I slam the door, I yell, "And why don't you clean up your mess in this room?"

I stand outside the door and realize that there's no private place to go . . . that Phoebe and I still have to share the room.

Maybe I should find a cave to live in alone. Life sure gets confusing when there's more than one person involved.

Jim and Mindy are in the kitchen talking, so I go into the living room.

I could ask to use Mindy's study, but then they'd ask what's the matter.

Sitting down on the couch, I look at the wall and see the picture of all of us at the Ulster County Fair.

Our happily ever after as a family lasted only one day.

9

It's war, all-out war.

In history class, we learned about the cold war.

In this house, it's the ice war.

Everyone's walking around incredibly tense.

No one's laughed or smiled in days.

It's all truly disgusting.

I baby-sit all the time.

Mindy's working overtime, waiting on tables.

Jim goes to his studio and tries to paint.

Phoebe spends most of her time with Dave. When he's working, she's on the phone or out with Beth Owen, a girl we both know. They're probably becoming best friends right now.

Phoebe walks into our bedroom.

She pretends that I'm not there.

I act like she's some giant cootie and stare at her, saying nothing while she brushes her hair.

She continues to ignore me.

This is more than truly disgusting.

It stinks.

There were reasons that we were best friends, lots of good ones.

In three days, it's as if there aren't any.

Something's got to give.

Someone's got to speak first.

Phoebe's stubborn.

I'm stubborn.

This could go on for the rest of our lives and someday, eighty years from now, we could wake up dead and never have spoken to each other.

It's like the thing with our beds, only more serious.

How come the adults can't straighten it out?

Someone's got to be reasonable.

How come it's got to be me who has to cope with stuff?

I hate to sound like a wimpette, but it's always me.

My parents get married, then divorced, and guess who got stuck dealing with the whole black/white issue. Me.

They both end up with people of their own color.

I'm like my own personal United Nations. Black. White.

Another thing that I've had to deal with is growing up without a lot of money. It's a good thing I love thrift-shop clothes.

The latest thing is this family war.

It looks like I'm going to have to give up being stubborn first.

If there's one thing I'm stubborn about, it's about giving up.

Phoebe stands up to leave.

It's now or never.

"Phoebe," I blurt out.

She turns to me and stands there.

"Please sit down," I say.

"Why?"

"We have to talk," I say.

"Why?"

"Come on." I speak softly. "We're friends— remember? Let's try to work it out."

She sits down and starts to cry. "I'm not sure that we can."

I sit down next to her. "We have to."

"It's not going to work out." Phoebe shakes her head.

"Can't you give it another chance?"

Phoebe says, "Mindy's got to apologize . . . get off my back . . . not tell me how to live my life."

I don't know what to do. I can't make Mindy apologize. I'm not even sure that she should if Phoebe doesn't also.

Phoebe continues. "I don't like this any better

than you do. How do you think I feel? My father won't even talk to me anymore unless I apologize. You and I are fighting. Do you think that I want to live like this?"

We both sit silently.

My brain hurts from trying to come up with a solution.

Finally, Phoebe sighs. "Tell them I'm willing to sit in on that family conference that they want. Tell them not to expect miracles. I'm not the one who has to apologize, but I'll be there."

"Why don't you tell them?" I ask.

She shakes her head. "I'll go to the conference. You tell them. Please."

It's a beginning, I think as I go downstairs to inform Jim and Mindy of this latest development. I only hope that the middle comes next, not the end.

10

"Welcome to our happy home." That's what I want to say as everyone sits down in the living room.

Somehow I don't think sarcasm is going to help, though.

It's five o'clock already, and it was hard enough figuring out where we'd meet.

Mindy thought it would be a good idea to sit around the dining-room table, since it's round and no one would be at the head of it.

Jim thought that was a bad idea. He grew up in a family where people yelled at each other all the time at meals while sitting around the table. In our house he wants us to feel good at the table.

Personally I wouldn't care if we held the family conference in the bathtub, fully dressed, as long as this mess got straightened out.

Mindy's sitting on a chair, working on a patchwork quilt. She only works on it when she's upset about something that she's done or something that's been done to her. Then she calls it her patchwork guilt. She's been working on it for years, off and on.

Phoebe's lying on her stomach, staring at her watch.

Jim's sitting crosslegged on a cushion on the floor, looking very serious.

I'm sitting in a wicker rocker.

Nobody's talking and it's driving me absolutely nuts.

Finally Jim begins. "I want everything to be all straightened out by the end of this meeting."

"And I want to be Queen of England. That's about as likely as everything working out." Phoebe glares.

"Maybe we shouldn't even waste our time." Mindy looks up from the quilt. "I'm getting sick and tired of what's been going on in this house and I'm not going to waste my time sitting here if nothing is going to be resolved."

There's silence again.

I can't think of anything to say to make it better.

Jim starts again. "Let's all try to get this worked out. . . . Phoebe, I want you to understand something. It was my fault that Mindy said anything. I got very angry that you were in front of our house, making out in broad daylight. I was going to go out to the car and yell, but Mindy persuaded me not to do that. She felt that it would embarrass you and Dave. She said that she would talk to you about it later. Protecting you was what Mindy wanted."

Phoebe looks at him and then at Mindy. She looks a little less angry.

Mindy puts down her sewing. "I was wrong to discuss the situation in a public place. I'm sorry for that."

Phoebe nods. "You were wrong."

Mindy sighs. "I just said that."

Damn it. Can't Phoebe give in one inch, just accept Mindy's apology without making her feel awful, and let us get on with our lives?

Phoebe looks at Jim. "We always worked things out by *ourselves*. You always get a little weirded out about my going on dates. But before Mindy came into your life, we did okay."

Jim quietly says, "Mindy came into our lives. In fact, we've all come into each other's lives and have to make adjustments."

I think about how I had to give up my dog and cat.

Phoebe shakes her head. "I'm always the one who has to make adjustments. I came home from camp and found out that you and Mom were getting a divorce. You both decided on joint custody. So I adjusted to spending half the week with you and the other half with Mom. I'm the one who had to go back and forth. You both stayed in your own places. Then you decided that I should leave all my friends at my old school, my old boyfriend, to move up here with you."

"You almost got thrown out of that school," Jim reminds her. "You glued everything down, remember?"

"I remember." Phoebe's crying. "I guess I didn't adjust so well after all."

Again there's silence and then Phoebe continues. "I was just really getting used to the new way and everything started to change again. My mother decides to marry a real creep. I had to adjust to that. Then you and Mindy decide to live together, to give up our wonderful house and the life I was finally used to. I'm supposed to adjust again."

"I thought we all got along well before," Mindy says.

"We did." Phoebe wipes her eyes. "But it's different with all of us under one roof. Why couldn't you wait until Rosie and I went away to college?"

"And put my life on hold for several years?" Jim slams his fist down. "You're being very self-centered."

"Bottom line," Phoebe says, "is that no matter

how I feel, you are going to do what you want, right?"

Jim thinks about that. "I'm going to try to do what's best for us, and right now I think it's best that we try to work this out and be a family."

"Come on, Phoebe," I say. "I really want this, don't you?"

She shrugs. "I don't know, Rosie. I just know that I want us to be best friends, but it was great the way it was before . . . our own houses, our own rooms. We don't even have enough room to put our clothes away. There's no privacy. And I can't even spend time with my boyfriend any-more without there being trouble."

Mindy looks at her. "And I can't even spend time with Jim without there being trouble. You're acting as if you are absolutely blameless."

Phoebe looks down at the carpet.

Mindy continues. "It's as if you are the only person in this family who has to make changes, as if you are the only one with anything at stake here. You know, Phoebe, I very carefully made the decision to make this change. It makes my life different too. I happen to love your father very much and want to be with him."

Phoebe says nothing.

Jim also is being very quiet.

Mindy says, "We're all living here together and will have to get used to that. What I really want is for all of us to be happy. Obviously, that's going to take some work."

It's kind of depressing. My fantasy's always been that everything would be so easy when we really found the right people to form a family with.

Jim says, "Look, Phoebe. From now on I'll communicate directly with you, not have Mindy do my dirty work for me."

Mindy looks at him. "You didn't have me do that. I did it on my own. I was wrong. I'm sorry. So I'm human and make mistakes. I definitely didn't do it out of meanness. What happens if I want to express my own feelings to Phoebe? Am I not supposed to do that? I refuse to accept the role of the wicked stepmother and I'm not going to be a wimp either and be afraid to say what I'm feeling."

"I don't want to be afraid to say what I feel either," Phoebe says.

It's so hard getting this mess straightened out. Maybe it would be better if we didn't live together.

"Can I go now? Dave's coming over soon." Phoebe looks at her watch.

Mindy stares at her. If looks could kill, Phoebe would be planted in the Donners' garden with the turtle.

Jim shakes his head. "Phoebe, you are doing everything you can to try to run this family. You can't do that."

Silence again.

Jim continues. "Nobody's leaving until you promise to try to work this out."

We could be here forever, I think.

Phoebe looks at her watch, though, and says, "I'll try."

Jim says, "Good. I knew I could count on you to be reasonable."

I'm not as sure of that as he is.

Mindy looks at her. "I want some time alone with you tomorrow, Phoebe, to talk some of this out calmly, sensibly, and privately. Do you think you can do that?"

Phoebe nods.

It certainly seems that a lot in this family is going to revolve around Phoebe. I certainly hope that they don't forget that I'm here and have feelings too.

Jim and Mindy walk out of the room. I'd love to hear their conversation about all this.

Actually, I probably wouldn't.

Coming up to me, Phoebe says, "Rosie, I'm sorry that we've had all this fighting. I don't want us to fight. You're my best friend. Please come to Canada with me. I never told Mom that you weren't coming or anything."

I'm not sure of what I want to do. Part of me wants to strangle her and the other part wants to make up.

She pleads. "I promise to try to work things out. Look, we'll really have fun. I promise.

Don't make me go to Canada alone with my mother and Duane."

"Are you really going to act differently from now on?" I look at her very closely.

She nods. "Yes. Now, please say yes. It'll be awful without you. I'm sorry for what I said to you, and I'll try to keep the room neater. Just say yes."

"I figured that you would have asked Beth by now."

She shakes her head. "No. She's my friend, too, but not like you are. You know how people always need a friend on the outside to talk to when there's trouble in the family. So I talked to Beth."

Another change. But at least Phoebe's talking about us as a family.

"Come on, Rosie. You're my sister." Phoebe looks like the Little Nerdlet does when he really wants something.

She likes having a family when she needs one, it seems.

I'll give it one more chance. I guess I want a family all the time.

I only wish we'd start living like one instead of having to talk it all out.

"I'll go," I tell her.

It's not so easy making happily ever after work.

11

"We're off to see the Gizard," Jim sings to the melody of the title song of *The Wizard of Oz.*

The four of us are driving down the New York Thruway on our way to La Guardia Airport.

Things have been going pretty well since the conference. It's not perfect, but everyone's trying.

"It's so embarrassing," Phoebe whispers to me. "He sings that every time we start out on a big trip. He thinks it's funny. Just wait till we get to our destination. Then he'll say, 'Well, Toto, I guess we're not in Kansas anymore.'"

"It could be worse," I say as Mindy joins in with the singing.

It is worse. She's got a terrible voice. She told me once that when she tried out for the high school glee club, the teacher told her to stop fooling around and sing in her normal voice. She was.

Phoebe continues. "Then after he does the Dorothy imitation, he's not done. Eventually he sticks out his finger like E.T. and says, 'Phone home.' He won't give up until I say it too. You'll see. It's so embarrassing. He does it in front of other people. Why can't he just remind me to call when I get there, like a normal person?"

"La Guardia Airport, coming up," Jim says, as he turns off the main road.

We arrive in front of the terminal.

As we open the car doors, Jim says, "Well, Toto, I guess we're not in Kansas anymore."

Phoebe and I look at each other and laugh.

The porter helps get the bags out of the car, and Jim drives off to park the car.

There's a medium bag for me, as well as a piece of carry-on luggage. I borrowed them from the Little Nerdlet's mother.

Phoebe's got two bags, plus a carry-on. She's got so much packed in hers: electric curlers, hair drier, portable Water Pik, eight pairs of shoes, pants, shirts, and lots of other stuff. She's also got a fold-up piece of luggage for the stuff she's going to buy.

The porter asks, "Want to check in these bags?"

"Yes," Mindy says.

"Tickets." He waits patiently.

"I don't have them." Mindy looks at Phoebe. "You do, don't you?"

Phoebe shakes her head. "I thought you had them."

The porter looks at me.

"Not I." I shake my head.

We all look at each other.

When Phoebe's mother and stepfather sent the tickets, we carefully put them in a safe place on the refrigerator.

I have a feeling that Mr. and Mrs. Carson should have held on to them until we got here. Sometimes I don't understand the way other people's brains work.

"When you get this straightened out, I'll come back," the porter says, going over to the curb to help someone else.

We all look at each other.

I hope this doesn't start more trouble between Mindy and Phoebe.

I start to giggle. Sometimes when I get really nervous I do that and can't stop. This problem has caused many detentions.

"I hope Dad's got the tickets." Phoebe shakes her head. "That's all Duane and Mom need to hear, that we don't have them. They think we're all weird and irresponsible anyway."

"They're wrong." Mindy is annoyed. "Just because we don't choose their life-style doesn't make us wrong."

I've got the giggling down to the point where it's sort of little inward hiccups. "Don't get so upset, Mindy. We've only misplaced the tickets, not Phoebe."

Mindy laughs. "You're right. I guess this meeting has me a little nervous."

"Mindy, don't worry. Mom's probably just as nervous as you," Phoebe offers. "Duane, however, probably wishes that he never had to deal with any of us."

Like the cavalry coming to save the situation, Jim arrives and saves the day. The tickets are in his hand.

Except for the carry-ons, the bags get checked in.

We enter the terminal. The place is jammed with people. I wish that I could know everybody's story . . . where they're going, who they're picking up. Since I don't know, I make up stories about them in my head.

I told Mindy how I love doing that. She says that's the sign of someone who writes. Maybe someday that's what I'll do . . . just like Mindy.

Everyone in our group is standing around talking. Not about anything important.

Everyone's really dreading meeting Phoebe's mother and stepfather at the departure gate. Of all of us, I'm the one who's got the least reason to feel nervous.

"We're going to be late," I tell them. "Come on, no more stalling."

We rush to the gate.

Mrs. Carson's pacing up and down.

She hugs Phoebe and says, "Where have you been?"

"Technical difficulties." Phoebe gives her a smile as she steps back.

"Hi, Kathy," Jim says, reaching out to shake her hand and then putting his hand down when she doesn't extend hers.

Mrs. Carson realizes what's just happened and reaches her hand out just as Jim finishes dropping his.

What confusion. They can't even get it together to shake hands. Obviously, they got it together at one point to do a whole lot more. Phoebe's proof of that.

It's kind of weird to watch ex-married people try to make contact when it's changed so much. Mindy and my father were like that for a while until they decided that they really hated each other and now have almost nothing to do with each other.

Mrs. Carson touches Jim on the arm.

Mindy stares at her.

"Jim, this is Duane."

The ex and present husbands meet and coolly shake hands.

"And this is Mindy." Jim goes over and puts his arm around Mindy's shoulder.

Kathy and Mindy smile at each other and say hello.

Jim continues. "Kathy. You know Rosie."

She smiles at me, gives me a hug, and introduces me to Duane, who shakes my hand and nods to Phoebe.

Then we all stand there, looking at each other, saying nothing.

I wonder what people waiting for the plane think of our strange group. I know that if I were watching and not involved, I'd sure be curious. Mindy looks beautiful, as always. Her outfit is very Woodstock—turquoise peasant skirt and blouse, Birkenstock sandals, and lots of beautiful Indian jewelry.

Jim's wearing denims, a black turtleneck, and sandals.

Phoebe's got on denims and a T-shirt that looks like it's from a college and says "Neurotic State."

I've got on denims and a black glitter-painted shirt.

Duane the Drip, who is pretending not to know us, is in a three-piece suit, even though the weather is warm.

I bet the observers are real confused about what I'm doing with this group.

It's time-warp time. The superstraights meet the post-hippies.

The woman at the desk announces that the

plane will be ready for boarding in a few minutes.

Jim turns to Phoebe, holds out his finger, and says, "Phoebe, phone home."

"Dad, please don't." Phoebe blushes.

He stands there, with his finger pointing.

Finally she smiles, holds out her finger and says, "Phoebe, phone home."

Jim does the same to me, and I respond.

Duane continues to act as if he doesn't know us.

As Mindy and I hug each other, she says, "Have a great time, honey. If you need me for anything, night or day, call collect. Promise."

I promise.

Mindy hugs Phoebe.

I hug Jim.

Then we say our goodbyes and walk toward the plane.

As we board, Mrs. Carson says to Phoebe, "Your father and 'Phone home.' Does he still sing 'We're off to see the Gizard'? "

Phoebe says yes and Mrs. Carson smiles.

I guess that not all of the memories are so terrible.

Well, we made it through our first meeting as what some people call an extended family.

I only hope that Toronto goes as well . . . if not better.

12

If you fail to declare—or falsely declare—
goods, they may be SEIZED and FOR-
FEITED and you may face prosecution.

"Uh-oh," I say after reading the form that the
flight attendant has given each passenger.

Phoebe looks up. "What's wrong?"

"I think the present Mindy bought to give our
hosts costs more than the amount allowed. I'm
in deep trouble. It'll be either taken or taxed. I
could end up in jail. What should I do?"

"I'll ask Mom and Duane."

"Not too loudly," I whisper.

Phoebe leans across the aisle to consult with
them.

Duane listens to her and then says, "Just say that it's under the limit. Rosie doesn't look like she'd be smuggling drugs or anything, even if she is from Woodstock."

Phoebe turns to me and crosses her eyes.

Duane's so obnoxious that he makes my step-mother look like an angel.

As for the lying—it's easy for him to say to do that. He won't have to spend his formative teen-age years languishing in prison.

I hide my face behind the paper and read the rest of the form. I am not to bring animals, birds, dairy products, plants, or soil into Canada. I check under my nails to make sure that there's no Woodstock dirt.

I do wish that Mindy had told me how much the present cost. I know it's a beautiful glass pa-perweight from Clouds, the Woodstock store that's like an art gallery. It was already gift wrapped when she brought it home.

Being arrested would be a real down in terms of my trip. It might come in handy, though, for those stupid assignments about "how I spent my summer vacation."

We're sitting in the first-class section, which is definitely a first for me.

The seats are larger and the service is great.

Mindy would definitely think it's an extrava-gance.

It's becoming clear how different it is for Phoebe to live in both places.

Mrs. Carson leans over and talks to us during the flight. Her husband reads *The Wall Street Journal* and doesn't say a word. Something tells me that if he knew the words "slug slime" he would use the phrase to describe Phoebe and me. He's probably too proper. He'd probably refer to us as "people pollution."

One hour and twenty minutes after the plane takes off, it lands. It took almost less time to get to a foreign country than it did to go from Woodstock to the airport.

After getting off the plane, we go down a long hall and arrive at this area where people are lined up waiting to go up to counters to talk to customs officials.

The signs explaining what to do are written in English and French.

I get in line behind the Carsons.

They get through quickly.

I hope to see them again.

I step up to the counter and try to look innocent.

The customs guy asks me if I have anything to declare.

I think of Butterfly McQueen's line from *Gone With the Wind*, "I do declare, Miss Scarlett . . ." But decide not to say it.

I'm not sure this guy's got a sense of humor.

I just say, "A little present." After all, the paperweight *is* tiny.

He lets me go through.

If there's a heaven, I hope that God didn't see me lying. I'd hate to be kept out for a paperweight.

We've actually arrived in Canada.

As we go out the doors into another area, I hear someone yell, "Duane, over here."

"Hello, Michael." Duane nods to his brother.

It's obvious that his brother was going to hug Duane but ends up nodding too.

Phoebe's absolutely right about Duane.

Introductions are made.

Mr. and Mrs. Carson hug us, saying that we should call them by their first names, Michael and Bev. They seem like nice people, sort of Woodstocky . . . casual and caring.

They're at least ten to fifteen years younger than Duane, more the age of Phoebe's and my parents.

We go out to the parking lot, then crowd into their car.

I'm actually in a foreign country.

As the car pulls out of the lot, I wonder why Duane's an American and his brother's Canadian.

Once before I asked Phoebe. She wasn't sure but said, "If you had Duane as an older brother, wouldn't you want to move to another country?"

Driving into Toronto, Michael points out some of the sights. The CN Tower stands over the city. Toronto is such a beautiful clean city.

There's a Chinatown and other ethnic areas. There are sections that look like suburbs with homes and little apartment buildings.

We travel along until we reach Russell Hill Road. Michael pulls into a long driveway and stops at a house that looks like an old English mansion.

"Home," he says.

Well, Phoebe, I guess we're not in Woodstock anymore.

13

"Oh, Rosie. I miss Dave so much I could die."

"You saw him yesterday," I remind her. "We just got here. We're unpacking."

"But my heart hurts, I miss him so much." Phoebe puts one hand to her forehead and the other to her heart.

She's been watching too many soap operas.

"Do you think that he's thinking of me at this very moment?" She swoons on the bed. "That our two hearts are throbbing in unison across the continent between the two nations?"

I may puke.

She sits up. "He's at work. I'll call him later."

Changing the subject, I say, "Isn't this house

incredible? Have you ever seen so many beautiful things in one place? It's so comfy and warm."

"The art, the pottery, antiques. It's great." Phoebe hangs up her clothes.

I guess she's neater visiting than living.

"Who would have thought that Duane would have human relatives?"

"I wonder what their kids are like." I finish putting my clothes in the dresser.

"We'll find out when they get back from their music lessons. Bev said that Jason's a little older than we are and Aviva's our age." Phoebe sits down on the bed. "Listen, Rosie, I'm really glad you're here."

"Me too."

"Rosie! Phoebe!" Bev calls up the stairs. "Jason and Aviva are here. Come on down to meet them."

Phoebe brushes her hair and says, "Well, let's check them out."

I put on some lipstick and say, "They'll be checking us out also."

She grins. "Oh . . . right. I wish you hadn't mentioned that."

We go down the stairs, Phoebe first, and enter the kitchen.

Aviva and Jason are emptying grocery bags.

They look like brother and sister. Brown hair. Brown eyes. Both are cute without being so attractive that you're afraid of them.

Jason in fact is very cute and seems very nice.

Phoebe notices.

She begins to flirt with him.

I wonder how Dave's heart is feeling right this second. I also wonder if I'll ever get over feeling shy around boys that I might like.

Phoebe asks him what sign he is.

I'm a goner if that's what it takes to have boys pay attention.

He grins. "My sign? . . . 'Slow Children at Play.' That's always been my favorite sign."

I laugh. "I've always liked the 'No Standing' sign. I feel guilty about being upright around one of them and wonder if I should lie down and roll through the area."

Jason looks at me and smiles.

Phoebe says, "The two of you are very silly."

We agree and then we all ask each other some questions to get to know each other, like school grade, interests, favorite ice cream flavors.

Aviva's a drummer.

Jason's a guitar player and singer.

Phoebe's standing right next to Jason, acting like he's the most important person in the world.

It's not fair. She's got Dave.

I hope she's not going to pair off with Jason. I'd really hate that.

I'm getting so good at pretending it doesn't matter that even I'm beginning to believe it.

14

"Time to go shopping." Mrs. Carson comes into the kitchen. "Bev and Aviva have promised to give us a guided tour of Eaton Center."

"Are you going too?" I'm glad that Phoebe asks Jason.

He shakes his head. "I hate malls."

That's something that we have in common. I would prefer to stay behind but it wouldn't be right, since Phoebe's mom and Plastic Pop paid for my trip.

Jason says, "See you later, I hope," and seems to look straight at me.

As we go out, Phoebe says in a surprised whisper, "He likes you. I can tell."

I say nothing and hope no one heard her. It

would be so embarrassing if someone did hear and Jason really didn't like me. Once, in the seventh grade, I had this tremendous crush on a boy and let him know. He acted really gross, ignoring me and making me feel like slug slime. Since then I've been sort of scared to show my feelings. In dating I guess I'm a late bloomer with an early inferiority complex.

Mrs. Carson and Bev are in the front of the car and we three kids sit in the back.

As the car heads to the mall, Aviva says, "I'm going to be your official tour guide. I did a school report on Eaton Center and I have lots of semi-useless information that I can give you."

Bev says, "Aviva's got a photographic memory."

"Oh, Mom." Aviva turns red.

Even moms who are great can be embarrassing.

We're just going to a shopping mall, I think. There's nothing so special about that. Shopping malls are all over the country. There're even some in Kingston, the city near Woodstock.

We get to Eaton Center and park.

Walking inside, I realize that it's not just any shopping mall.

Aviva begins. "This place is 300,000 square meters. That's over three million square feet in American. Fifteen thousand people work here."

"That's more people than live in Woodstock, even in the summer." I shake my head.

The place is really something. There are glass-enclosed elevators. There's a fountain that's timed to shoot water up in the air at certain times in certain patterns. It reminds me of trying to toilet-train the Little Nerdlet.

Aviva takes a deep breath and continues. "There are fifty fashion stores, more than two dozen shoe stores, more than sixty restaurants, fast-food outlets, and specialty food shops. There are also twenty-one movie theaters."

I think of the Tinker Street Cinema back in Woodstock. It holds 162 people.

Phoebe grins. "I could live in this place. Let's start checking out some of the stores."

We take the elevator up to the mall's third floor and go into a very ritzy-looking store.

Phoebe and her mother immediately start trying on clothes.

Everything is designer-labeled and designer-priced. I don't even like the clothes. They're not my style.

Sitting on a chair, I watch as they all look in the mirrors.

Mrs. Carson comes over and says, "Rosie. Pick out an outfit. I'd love to get it for you."

"Thanks. But there's nothing here for me." I smile at her.

They continue to try on clothes.

Phoebe's smiling. "This is so fun."

Mrs. Carson looks at her. "Honey, if you lived

with us in New York, we'd be able to shop all the time. And the schools are so much better."

"Mom," Phoebe says.

"And you'd have your own room," Mrs. Carson continues.

I'll just take the knife out of my heart right now, I think.

"Mom." Phoebe makes a face. "I don't want to talk about that now."

I notice that she's said "now."

They continue to try on clothes.

Phoebe always used to make fun of the way her mother dresses. It's weird that she's so into shopping at this store.

Aviva comes over and sits down beside me. "I'm tired of this already. Why don't we say that we'll meet them for lunch and go visit some of the other places that are more fun?"

"Great idea." I nod.

We tell them and make arrangements to meet them for lunch at a place called Mr. Greenjeans and head out the door.

Going into a store with lots of stickers and fun things, I find the perfect Christmas present for the Little Nerdlet. It's a pair of earmuffs with each side shaped like mouse heads. I just know that the Little Nerdlet's going to love it. Even though it's only August, I buy it to give him in December.

Walking into another place, I ask Aviva about

why her family is Canadian and Duane is American.

She stops to try on a pair of earrings. "My father's much younger than Duane, and his politics are different. During the Vietnam War, my father was going to be drafted if he stayed in the United States. So he and Mom moved to Canada. They had a rough time of it. His family wouldn't talk to him. He was a fugitive. And then by the time the U.S. offered amnesty, he decided to stay and become a Canadian citizen. He did go back for a while to work it out so that he could go to the U.S. without being arrested. And he kind of made up with his family."

"That's a great story," I say. "He should write it down. I would if it happened to me."

"He's not a writer." Aviva smiles. "He loves working with computers."

It's amazing. Duane and his brother are both into computers and they're so different.

"I'm not great with computers." I laugh. "Last year in school I was having lots of trouble getting my program to work and I got angry. So I typed in some profanity, telling the computer what to do with its bytes."

"What happened?" Aviva smiles.

"It printed out 'Please don't use such bad language. I'm only a machine and I can't take it.' "

"Is that true?" Aviva is doubled over laughing.

I nod. "Then I tried all sorts of other words

on it and the computer said the same thing.
Some teacher must have programmed it in."

"Can you imagine?" Aviva still can't stop
laughing. "The teacher probably tried to write
in every possible combination of words that a
student could use to swear. I thought teachers
weren't supposed to know bad words."

When we finally calm down, it's time to meet
Phoebe, Mrs. Carson, and Bev for lunch.

We go to Mr. Greenjeans. They're already
there. We order hamburgers. They turn out to
be the largest I've ever seen.

"Where were you?" Phoebe asks.

We tell her and show her the Little Nerdlet's
present.

She's got several packages next to her but
doesn't show us what's in them.

Phoebe doesn't seem too pleased that Aviva
and I went off without her.

What else should we have done? Been bored
with waiting until she picked out her little de-
signer outfits? When we said that we were going,
she didn't say she wanted to come with us.

She's very quiet. Too quiet.

I refuse to feel guilty. Enough is enough. I
know I was brought along to keep her company,
but she was busy buying clothes. That was time
to spend with her mother—which was the real
reason for this trip. Sometimes I think that the
only time those two communicate is when
they're shopping.

I look at Phoebe and try hard to make contact. "We passed a store called Perry's. They take pictures of people dressed in old-time clothes. Why don't the three of us go there after lunch and have a picture taken?"

"You and Aviva . . . and me?" Phoebe looks at us.

I stare at her. "The three of us. . . . Don't be silly. . . . You know that I want you in the picture."

She holds up a french fry to her face and pretends that it's a moustache.

Now she's acting like the Phoebe that I know and love . . . my best friend—sort of sister.

After finishing lunch, we go over to Perry's. With Bev and Mrs. Carson cheering us on, we dress up.

I'm wearing a 1920s Charleston dress and long beads, and I'm carrying a beaded bag.

Phoebe's wearing a Victorian dress with lots of ruffles and holding a rose.

Aviva's dressed in a 1950s skirt with a poodle emblem and a fluffy angora sweater.

We all look like we've come from very different eras and met in the present.

The photographer snaps the pictures.

We change, visit some other stores, and come back in half an hour. The pictures are really great. Each of us gets one.

We all look different, individual, and yet in a funny way, a team.

I hope we can maintain that feeling for the entire visit without anyone feeling jealous or left out.

Life sure can get complicated when you're supposed to be having fun.

15

"It's R night at the movies tonight," Jason says, as we all sit down for dinner.

Duane objects. "I don't think you children should choose to go to a movie simply because of its rating."

Jason explains that the Canadian movie rating system is different from ours and, anyway, that's not what he meant.

The Carsons fill us in.

Michael starts. "When we bought the six-foot projection screen, our house became very popular."

Aviva laughs. "Kids I didn't even know were coming up to me and asking if they could come over."

"The football coach asked if he could bring the team over to view the videos of the game." Jason shakes his head. "I'm not even on the team."

"And the cheerleaders wanted me to film them at the games and then invite them over," Aviva says. "Instant Insincere Popularity."

"We just invite our friends over, the real ones . . . but try to keep it manageable," Jason says.

"Now a lot more kids have giant screens but our house is still a hangout because the kids seem comfortable here. We do have rules," Bev informs us. "Every couple of months the kids can have a dance party where videos are shown. Once a month the kids can have an all-night film party."

I think I could handle rules like that.

Jason continues. "We decided to show the films alphabetically. The first party had films starting with the letter A. Now we're up to R— so tonight's R night. We debated rescheduling because you were coming but thought that Rosie and Phoebe might enjoy it."

Phoebe and I grin at each other.

"Will this party be chaperoned? Won't it be noisy? How will anyone get any sleep? I hope there will be no drinking or drugs." Duane demands answers.

Michael shakes his head. "No drugs or alcohol. That's one of our rules. You know, Duane, you sound like you did when I was a kid . . .

always questions asked with obvious disapproval."

Duane looks angry but doesn't say anything.

I put down my fork and stop eating.

Michael looks like a kid who's not sure if he's going to get yelled at but not ready to back down.

Families. I guess some of the problems last for a long time.

Mrs. Carson puts her hand on Duane's and pats it.

Finally Duane speaks. "Michael, there's a big age difference between us and I've always felt a little responsible. I wanted to protect you. After all, you did get into a lot of trouble when you were a kid."

Michael nods. "The trouble that I got into was because I believed in what I was doing. It was necessary to make those in power understand that there had to be changes."

"You were jailed," Duane reminds him.

Michael says, "And proud of it. I was jailed for demonstrating against actions I thought were immoral. And the demonstrations made a difference."

I think of Mindy and wonder whether she and Michael were ever at any of the same demonstrations.

Bev says, "Come on, you two. You promised not to discuss this anymore."

The brothers look at each other and then nod.

What a relief. A truce.

Bev says, "Duane, don't worry about the noise. The kids are pretty quiet and the projection TV is not in the wing where the adult bedrooms are."

"What are we going to see?" I ask.

Jason smiles at me. "We decided on *Raiders of the Lost Ark, Rear Window, Reds, The Red Shoes,* Roadrunner cartoons, and videos of the Rolling Stones."

"It sounds great," Phoebe says. "I wish my boyfriend Dave was here. He'd love to see all of that."

She's mentioned Dave for the first time in front of Jason. Very interesting. I guess she's decided not to make a play for him.

After dinner Phoebe, Aviva, Jason, and I clear the table.

At one point I'm all alone in the dining room.

Jason walks in and comes up to me. "I'm in charge of making the popcorn tonight. How about helping me out. . . . I realize that this is a pretty 'corny' way to ask you out."

I almost drop the plates but try to look as if it's an everyday occurrence that I'm asked on a popcorn date by a very nice, cute guy.

"Okay." I nod. "I'd love to . . . although there's a kernel of truth in your saying that it's corny."

He groans and grins.

I like a guy who can groan and grin at the same time, especially since I love puns.

Phoebe walks in as we're grinning at each other. She goes over to the table, clears more dishes, and leaves without saying anything.

Jason and I continue to smile.

Finally he says, "Would you like some help in carrying those dishes?"

I hand half of them to him.

As we walk into the kitchen, he says, "If we're going to make the popcorn, we'd butter hurry up and finish clearing the table."

Now I know I'm in love. He's nice, cute, and punny.

And we have four days left to get to know each other.

16

Tonight is the best night of my life—almost.

Who would have guessed that making popcorn could be so much fun?

Jason is the nicest, most wonderful boy in the world.

There hasn't even been time to see the movies. Jason and I have been talking all night.

Kids walk in and out to get popcorn and soda. Only in Canada they call it soft drinks. I asked for soda and got tonic water. Bleech!

The *almost* best night is because of Phoebe. It would be perfect if she didn't keep coming in and asking that I sit with her at the movies.

"Soon," I keep saying. I'm having such a great time with Jason that I don't want to leave.

Finally, Phoebe walks into the kitchen, stamps her foot, and says, "I'm going to bed. Don't try to stop me."

Although I didn't plan to stop her, I do follow her out of the room to ask, "What's wrong?"

"Nothing's wrong," she says, and walks away in a huff.

I start to follow her, then decide not to. If she says nothing's wrong, I'll pretend that I believe her. With her temper tantrum, she's making me feel like a baby-sitter.

Walking back into the kitchen, I see that Jason is talking to some girl, so I don't go over to him.

I pretend to be very interested in rearranging the magnetic letters on the refrigerator to spell my name. By the time I've finished putting the N on WILSON, Jason comes up beside me.

He puts I REALLY LIKE above my name and then turns me around, putting his arms around my neck. He says, "Don't let Phoebe get you down. Mom thinks she's going through a really tough time because of her mother's remarriage."

Jason's just said that he likes me and he's got his arms around my neck.

Be still my heart.

I try to be calm and continue the conversation.

"Her father and my mother getting together has also made her a little bonkers."

He nods.

We just look at each other.

There's no more talk about Phoebe.

Someone walks in and asks for popcorn.

"Make it yourself," Jason tells him.

We just keep staring at each other.

Aviva comes into the kitchen. "The Rolling Stones video is on. Dance time."

"Want to?" Jason asks.

I nod yes, figuring that he's asking me to dance but ready for more hand-holding if that's what he means.

We go into the other room and dance.

He's a good dancer. I like the way he moves his body.

Uh-oh . . . I'm not sure I should be thinking about that.

The dancing goes on until the end of the video and then people sit down to watch *Reds*.

At 6:00 A.M., when the films end and people go home, Jason and I kiss goodnight . . . and then good morning. And then he asks me to spend the day with him.

"Yes," I say.

We each head to our own rooms for a nap, planning to meet in a couple of hours.

When I get into bed, I think about how I've finally met a boy who I really like who likes me.

I also think about how nice it was to kiss him.

I hope that he feels the same way.

Maybe I'm not the best kisser in the world, but I have a feeling that I could get better with practice.

I'm so excited that I think I'll never fall asleep but I must, because the next thing I hear as I wake up is Phoebe saying "Rosie, are you awake?"

"Now I am." I yawn.

"I want to talk to you." Phoebe is sitting up on her bed.

It's probably one of the first times that she's gotten up before me.

Sitting up, I say "Okay."

She's holding on tight to her pillow, which I hope is not going to turn into a weapon.

"Rosie, I thought you were here to be with me," she says.

"I am with you." I look at her. "Can't I talk to other people?"

"You've spent a lot of time with other people. First with Aviva and then with Jason. I felt all alone."

"I don't understand. In Woodstock, we're not together all the time. You're with Dave a lot. You're with other friends. There were a lot of kids to talk to last night." I try to reason with her.

Phoebe looks sad. "You make friends easier than I do. My friends in Woodstock are the ones you introduced me to when I moved there."

I never realized that Phoebe felt that way.

She continues, "It's also easier for me to deal with my mother and Duane with you here."

"But you got along well with your mother

yesterday . . . and aren't you supposed to spend the day shopping with her today?"

Phoebe nods. "Yes, it's not as bad as I thought it would be, but it helps to know you're there in case it goes badly."

I think about my date today with Jason and know that there's going to be trouble when Phoebe finds out.

"Look," I say. "It's good for you to be with your mother and work things out. . . . Also, I would like to spend the day with Jason. . . . He asked me out."

"You're going out with him?"

I nod.

"But you're supposed to be with me." She pouts.

It's so confusing. She's right. I was brought here to be with her, but I've also met Jason and want to spend some time with him. It really is the first time ever that I've met a boy like him.

I don't understand Phoebe anymore. She used to be different. She was my very best friend, and now sometimes I'm not even sure that she cares about me for *me*.

"What do you want me to do?" I ask. "Pay you back for the airplane flight? Go home now?" I stare at her. "Spend every second with you? Ask permission to go to the bathroom by myself?"

"I'm not that bad," Phoebe says.

"You are." I glare. "You're driving me nuts. I

want to say stuff to you like 'You know, Lincoln supposedly freed the slaves.' "

She gasps. "Oh, Rosie. . . . That's awful."

I nod.

She sits quietly.

Finally she says, "I'm so confused. Everything's different."

"You mean like some boy likes me and I'm not the one alone for once?" I'm really fed up.

She puts the pillow down on the bed. "I mean, like all of a sudden there's so much change in my life that I don't know how to act anymore."

"You act as if no one else in the world is going through anything but you. Lots of kids have to deal with divorces and repairings. I have to learn to act differently, too, but I'm willing to try. Why can't you?"

Phoebe shakes her head. "It's easier for you."

I shake my head. It makes me angry that when she has to go through something she thinks it's so hard. When I do it, it's supposed to be a breeze. . . . Wrong. Growing up's not easy for anyone.

Finally Phoebe says, "I'll try to work this out . . . somehow. . . . Don't worry about me."

I nod.

As we get up and dress, I think about how Phoebe's managed to make me unhappy when things should be so good. I know that I'll worry about her even though I say I won't. I'm also very angry.

A person should never have to choose between a best friend and a boy.

A person should never have to choose between a best friend and her own mother.

Phoebe's been trying to have me make a lot of unnecessary choices.

I'm trying to be reasonable, but it's getting very hard lately.

17

When I was little, I always wanted a Prince Charming to show up at my door and whisk me away to his castle.

My wanting the Prince and the castle come from watching all of those old Walt Disney movies. One of my favorites was the one where the birds dressed Cinderella. I'd always wanted that —until Mindy reminded me that the birds would probably leave droppings on the dress and on me.

Still there's something about a prince and castle that sounds very exciting.

Last night I told Jason about my fantasy and he said that he'd plan our date around it.

So here we are riding in his car on the way to somewhere.

I only hope it's not a bird store.

We pull up to a castle. Five minutes from Jason's house, there's a stone castle with towers and turrets.

Jason pulls into the driveway past the stone wall and into the parking lot.

"Amazing. I can't believe it."

He parks the car, then turns to me and says, "Casa Loma—the house on the hill."

He's so proud of himself.

He's also so cute . . . all six feet of him . . . his broad shoulders . . . the freckles on his pale face . . . the way he laces his shoes starting in the middle going to the bottom and then letting the laces hang. . . .

I don't think it's a good idea to keep staring at him . . . even though he keeps looking at me.

I start to open the door and jump out of the car to get a better look at the castle.

The safety belt is still locked. How embarrassing.

Jason unlocks it and we get out of the car.

He puts his arm around my shoulder.

I look up at him. "What's a castle doing in the middle of Toronto?"

Jason explains. "This guy Pellatt made a lot of money putting up streetlights in Toronto and investing in stuff. He had a thing about castles and decided to build one here."

"It must have cost a fortune." I look around at the wall, the stable across the street, and then back at the building.

"They started building it in 1905. By the time it was finished it cost three and a half million dollars."

With that kind of money, Mindy could quit waitressing and write full-time. Jim wouldn't have to worry about finances either.

"Incredible." I shake my head. "Pellatt must really have felt like a king."

"He went bankrupt in 1923 and had to leave the castle," Jason tells me.

"Wow. My mother's always telling me to put some money away for a rainy day. Pellatt could have prepared for a flood with what this place cost."

"For a long time this place was empty, and then in 1936 the Kiwanis Club took over and now it's a tourist attraction. The money they make goes to helping people," Jason says. "Want to see the inside of the place?"

"I'd love to."

Walking toward the castle with his arm around me, I try to relax and not trip. It's not so easy to walk with a tall person attached.

Jason pays the entrance fee and we're handed a map and information sheet.

As we walk inside, he says, "Let's pretend it's our castle."

"A great idea," I say.

The castle has ninety-eight rooms. The plan called for three bowling alleys, twenty-five fireplaces, an indoor swimming pool, and thirty bathrooms.

Thirty bathrooms—all I want in Woodstock is two.

Jason and I are holding hands as we walk through Casa Loma.

A lot of my attention is on our hands and the fact that we are touching.

We go through the billiard room. The information sheet says it was used by males only for smoking and games.

"That's sexist," I say. "If this is our castle, we should get rid of the smoke but let everyone play the games."

"Billiards." Jason laughs.

I shrug. "We'll put in video games."

We go through the rest of the castle—a library with room for ten thousand books, museum rooms, secret entrances, a wine cellar with room for seventeen hundred bottles, and my favorite room, the conservatory.

As we walk up the steps, we are very close to each other. The sides of our legs are almost touching.

Turning left, we are in the Norman tower with an incredible view of Toronto. We can also see the stables.

There's no one else up here but us.

I forget to look at Toronto and stare instead at him.

We keep looking at each other.

He leans forward and gives me a tiny kiss, sort of like he's trying to catch my lips in his.

Again he kisses me, this time for a little longer.

We separate, looking at each other again.

I love his brown eyes.

I love his smile.

I kiss him this time.

We hug each other tightly.

He kisses me on the top of my head.

I kiss him on his neck.

Tourists arrive at our tower.

We separate from each other.

I hate tourists.

From the tower we go to the gift shop so that I can get some postcards to send to friends.

There are some incredible things for sale. Jason and I keep holding things up that are hysterical.

There are some things that I have to take home. For Mindy I buy this ugly ceramic chicken. In the front on a little tray is a place for rings. Coming out of the chicken's rear end are measuring spoons. "Spooning for you at Casa Loma" is written on the chicken. Mindy's going to die when she sees it. She's really into tacky to make her laugh.

I buy Jim a large pink pencil with a globe of

the world on it. That's because he's always saying that it's hard to get the point of world politics.

Jason buys me a snow scene of Casa Loma, "So you'll always remember our day here."

As if I could ever forget this.

I buy Jason a ruler with scenes of Casa Loma on it. "Whenever you use this, you'll know that you're a real prince—a true ruler."

He laughs.

As we walk out to the car, I say, "I love our castle."

"And your prince?" he asks, taking my hand.

"And my prince." I nod, feeling a little shy.

He stops by the car. "What if you kiss the prince . . . and he turns into a frog?"

"Not a chance. I've already kissed you and you're not a frog." I look at his face.

"Are you sure?" He puts his hands on my shoulders. "Maybe you better check to make sure."

We check.

He doesn't turn into a frog.

I hope this day goes on forever.

18

"Harbourfront is one of my favorite places," Jason says as we walk near Lake Ontario.

"The stores. The restaurants. The theaters. I love it." I take out a pair of 1950s sunglasses that I found at a flea market and put them on to keep the sun out of my eyes.

As we look out at the water, Jason puts his hands on my shoulders. "Rosie Wilson, I'm so glad you came to Canada."

"Me too." My mouth feels like it's going to break from how wide my smile is.

While we look at each other, some guy comes up and says with hate, "Why don't you stick to your own kind?"

I can't believe it.

He repeats what he's just said.

Jason turns to him. "We are the same kind—human. You're the one who isn't our kind. You're scum."

The guy says something disgusting.

I want to throw up.

Jason moves toward him.

I grab Jason's arm and say, "Please, don't."

The woman who is with the creep says, "Harold, let's go. Don't start anything again. They're just kids."

Jason puts his arm around me, differently this time, like he wants to protect me.

"Let's go," I whisper. "Please."

Jason turns me around and we head to a restaurant.

The slug slime yells some bad names at us but he doesn't follow.

I'm so embarrassed. This is one of the worst moments in my life.

I'm glad I'm wearing sunglasses. Maybe Jason won't see the tears coming out of my eyes.

We sit down at a table.

Jason wipes the tears off my face. "Are you all right?"

"I think so." The tears keep coming. "Mindy's tried to prepare me for this kind of stuff, but I guess you can't know what it's like until it happens. My mother said that when she was married to my father, she had to deal with stuff like that. Someone once spit on her." I shake my head. "I've never had anyone talk to me like that man did."

"I bet he's a tourist, not a Canadian," Jason says. "Don't think we're like that."

I think of Jason's family and friends. I know they're not.

The waitress comes by and takes our order.

I'm not hungry but order something, sort of like a rent payment for using the table.

It's so embarrassing to be crying in public.

Jason rips the straw wrapper to bits. "I've been brought up to be a pacifist . . . and I wanted to kill that guy."

"Maybe it's not a good idea for us to go out." I sniffle.

"Wrong. It's a good idea. In fact, it's a great idea. You're the best girl I've ever met." Jason starts on another straw wrapper. "Has anything like this ever happened before?"

"No."

"See? Then he's just one piece of garbage. Not everyone's like him." Jason puts down the wrapper and takes my hand. "People like him don't fit into the way our world is now. He's got a brain like a dinosaur, and they became extinct. His kind will too."

"I hope so," I tell Jason. "It's weird. In Woodstock I've never had to think about it much. I do know when I visit my father, I meet some people who don't like white people, and when I'm with Mindy's parents and some of their friends, I know they would like it better if I were totally white. But nothing like this has ever happened before. . . . I really like being a combination of both colors and cultures."

"I think you have a lot of culture, and I love your skin color." Jason blushes. "It's beautiful."

"I love yours too." I blush, too, but it doesn't show as much. "But Jason, it's your freckles that are the same color as I am, not the rest of your skin."

"The freckles and my skin make me more than one color too," Jason teases. "You just blend better than I do. I spot."

That makes me laugh. It's good to know that I still remember how.

It's odd. Mindy's white and living now with a white man. My father's black and married to a black woman. Unless I'm with them, when they go out in public they don't have to deal with some of the stuff I may have to. Somehow, it's never been a big deal before. I hope it doesn't become one.

That guy deserves something awful to happen to him. He has no right to be like that. I bet when he was a kid he was one of those awful ones who thought that making fun of people made him a big shot.

I'm glad I'm growing up in a time when there are less of his kind around.

It still hurts though.

But I'm not going to let what happened mess things up between Jason and me.

Good princes are hard to find.

19

Phoebe's a real down.

Jason and I tried to include her in some of our plans. He even got one of his friends to take her out last night so we could double.

What a pill she was. No smiling. No talking.

The double date ended at about 9:30. When we came back to the house, she went upstairs and her date left. I felt bad for him. He was just trying to do Jason a favor. She didn't have to marry him, but she could have acted like a human being.

The good news was that Jason and I had some time alone.

I almost called Mindy collect to talk. So much has happened in just a little while. When I left she said that I could call, so she must have had a feeling that there might be problems.

I decided to wait because we'll be home later today.

Today. That means we're leaving Canada. I'm leaving Jason.

Last night we promised to write every day, to not forget each other, not that I ever could. He promised to come to Woodstock for Christmas.

As I pack I think about how much I'll miss him. How I like his smile. His sense of humor. The way he treats me. How he makes me feel. The way he kisses.

So much has happened. It's going to take a while to sort it all out.

"Breakfast." Aviva sticks her head in the door.

"I'll be ready in a few minutes."

She comes into the room. "I'm going to miss you, Rosie. Even if Jason did monopolize your time here, I really like you."

"Me too." I give her a hug.

"Why don't you come back here again soon?" she says. "You don't have to come up with them. You can come up on your own. I've already asked my parents, and they've said yes."

That makes me feel great.

Something tells me that Aviva is not happy with her relatives though.

I guess that includes Phoebe, who is off somewhere talking to her mother.

We go downstairs.

Jason is waiting for me at the bottom of the steps.

Aviva goes into the kitchen.

Jason and I hug each other.

I wonder how many days there are until Christmas vacation.

This is the last meal before the plane ride.

I can hardly bear leaving Jason.

Aviva comes out. "I hate to do this to you, but breakfast is being served."

We go in and sit at the table.

Phoebe's sitting quietly next to her mother.

Michael brings out his specialty, eggs Benedict.

He's so proud of his cooking.

He should be. It's great.

As we eat, I keep peeking over at Jason.

He's doing the same to me.

Once I cross my eyes just to throw him off guard.

He chokes on his eggs Benedict but quickly recovers.

Bev smiles at us and says, "Ah, young love."

Really embarrassing.

Duane starts talking about the state of the world economy.

Boring.

Phoebe's saying nothing, playing with her food with her fork.

She's even more boring than Duane.

Mrs. Carson starts to talk. "Listen, everyone. I have a wonderful announcement."

We all look at her. She's very happy.

Everyone stops talking and looks at her.

She smiles. "I'm so happy. I have the best news. Phoebe has decided to move back to New York to live with us. Isn't that wonderful?"

Wonderful isn't the word for it.

I guess this is what people mean by dropping a bombshell.

How could Phoebe do this without talking to me first?

Has she gone crazy?

Is she so angry at me for being with Jason that she's doing this to get back at me?

Is this a plot of her mother's?

How's Jim going to take this?

What will Mindy say?

I look around at everyone at the table.

No one's saying anything except Mrs. Carson.

She's the only one smiling.

Phoebe's not.

Nor is Duane.

Neither am I.

20

Jason's driving me to the airport.

Phoebe and the Carsons are in the other car with Bev and Michael.

There wasn't room for all of us in the same car and I'm glad.

I'm so angry at Phoebe for deserting our family.

There's so little time left to be with Jason. I don't want to waste it thinking about Phoebe.

Jason parks the car and says, "Once you go through customs, we'll have to separate."

I miss him already.

He reaches over and takes a package out of the glove compartment. "Here, Rosie. Unwrap this now."

It's in aluminum foil. Something tells me he wrapped it himself.

I tear the paper off.

It's a beanbag frog, made out of green material with yellow and black eyes and a zipper mouth.

"Kiss it," he says.

"I'd rather kiss you." I do.

In a few minutes he says, "Kiss the frog. We're going to be late for the plane otherwise, and I really want you to see this."

I kiss the frog.

Jason takes it from me, unzips the mouth and turns it inside out.

Zipping it back up, he shows it to me.

Now it's a prince.

"Jason, I love it. It's the best present in the whole world."

He's very proud of himself.

I put the frog/prince in my travel bag.

We kiss and then rush to the customs area, where everyone else is waiting.

Duane and Mrs. Carson don't look too pleased, but at this point, who cares.

It's awful to say goodbye, especially in front of everyone.

I'm also going to miss his parents and Aviva.

Once we answer the customs guy's questions, we have to go.

I can hardly stand it.

Next thing I know, the Carsons, Phoebe, and I are in a room waiting for the plane.

I say nothing, thinking of Jason.

I sneak a peek in my travel bag and touch the frog/prince.

Normally I would have shown it to Phoebe, but I'm not sure that I want to share anything with her right now.

Once we get on the plane, I take out a magazine and pretend to be engrossed in it.

We haven't said anything to each other since her mother's announcement.

Finally I can't stand it anymore. "Phoebe, how could you? Why are you moving?"

She's got a very removed attitude and a cold voice. "New York has so much more to offer."

"But you've always said that you liked Woodstock better."

She stares ahead. "That was when I was younger."

"Two months ago," I remind her.

Continuing, she says, "There's much more to do in New York City . . . so many cultural advantages . . . the theater . . . first-run films . . . a higher-quality school system."

Either Phoebe's been taken over by an alien inhabiting her body or she's been listening to her mother too much.

"What about Dave?" I want to know. "What about me?"

For a minute there's this flicker of feeling like she's not a robot. "I'll miss Dave, but we'll still see each other. He can come down to the city

and I'll still be coming up to Woodstock sometimes. I'll just be riding the Divorce Express in
reverse. So Dave and I will see each other. So
will you and I."

I want to pound her on the head with the air-
line magazine but decide not to create a scene,
especially not in first class.

"What about Jim? How do you think your father's going to feel about this?" I roll up the
magazine.

She shrugs. "He's got Mindy. He won't miss
me."

How disgusting can she get?

That's it. I stop asking questions.

The rest of the plane ride takes place in silence.

When the plane lands, I check to make sure
that the frog/prince is still in the travel bag and
quickly rush off the plane to find Mindy and
Jim.

They're right where I thought they would be,
waiting for us at the front of a crowd.

I knew I could depend on them to be there.

As we're picking up our luggage, Mrs. Carson
says to Jim, "We have something important to
talk out. If you would be so kind, Phoebe,
Duane, and I have something to talk to you
about. We need to work out some arrangements
with you."

Poor Jim. He doesn't have any idea of what's

coming. How cruel. How can they do this to him this way?

Mindy looks at him. "Honey, if you want, Rosie and I will go for a cup of coffee so that you can talk. You can meet us in the restaurant after you're done."

Mindy gives him a kiss and whispers something to him.

I know she's checking to see if he wants her to come along for moral support.

He shakes his head and returns her kiss.

As they head off for their discussion, Mindy turns to me and says, "What's going on?"

I explain.

"Poor Jim," Mindy says softly. "This is going to tear him apart. . . . Phoebe must be even angrier than we thought about us living together."

"Do you think he'll leave us to make her happy?" I ask.

Mindy hugs me. "Let's not think about that."

While we're waiting for them to return, I tell her all about Jason. Then I show her the frog/prince.

"He sounds like a nice boy." Mindy smiles but she seems a little distracted.

I do understand why she can't pay full attention to me right now, but I wish she could. There's so much I want to tell her, so much I want to ask her.

I also want to talk to her about what happened with that slug slime's comment about my color.

Something tells me that this is not the right time.

Jim and Phoebe come over to our table.

"Time to go home." Jim looks grim. "There's some packing to do."

No one says a word during the entire trip back to Woodstock.

I debate trying to start a conversation but know it won't do any good.

This is definitely not the time for a few choruses of "We're Off to See the Gizard."

Well, Phoebe, I guess you're not in Woodstock anymore.

21

Life goes on.

I guess.

I miss Jason so much.

We write, not every day, but lots.

Phoebe's enrolled back at her old school in New York.

Dave's so sad.

I'm not sure that I am.

Jim's a wreck. He walks around feeling responsible.

Mindy's upset because Jim's in such bad shape.

Even though Phoebe's not living with us, it's like she is.

She's coming up next weekend to visit.

There's still a bed for her in the room that I now consider mine.

I've used all of the storage space but one drawer, which she can use.

She better not be as sloppy as she used to be, because the room is very neat now.

She's not going to be too pleased that I've taken down her posters, even the one I liked.

Who cares? It's been over a month since Phoebe's left and next week will be her first visit.

Never has she written or called me.

The only one she's in regular contact with is Dave. She's only coming up here to go to a dance with him.

I'm going to stay at the Little Nerdlet's house on that weekend so that I won't have to see her face.

Mindy's upset that I'm leaving. "Rosie, it's your home. You shouldn't have to go."

However, she also said, "There's a part of me that wants to leave, too, but I'm not going to give her that satisfaction. I'll just work a double shift."

We refer to Phoebe as "she" and "her" a lot.

I'm lying on my bed, doing my Spanish homework with my stereo on full blast.

Last night was truly boring . . . another Saturday night with the Little Nerdlet . . . El Nerdleto Chiquito.

There's loud knocking on my door.

"Come in," I yell.

The door opens and Jim walks in, holding his ears.

I turn the music down.

"Rosie." He smiles at me. "I'm going for a ride to look at the leaves turning color and I'd love company. Want to go with me?"

I look down at my Spanish grammar book and decide to check out the leaves. "Sure. I'd love to."

Jim grins. "Great. I'll meet you at the car in five minutes, okay?"

After he goes, I put my books away, turn the stereo off, and think about how Jim and Phoebe always went out for rides in the fall.

As I go down the steps, I hear the sound of typing coming from Mindy's study.

Going outside, I see that Jim's already in the car.

As I get inside, he says, "How about Cooper Lake?"

"Great," I say.

Jim sings "Autumn Leaves," off tune but happily.

It's a good thing he's an artist, not a rock singer.

Cooper Lake is beautiful. The clear blue water, the leaves turning red, orange, and shades of green.

I wonder what it's like at Lake Ontario and wish I could be there with Jason or he could be here with me.

We drive around for a while and then head for Sunfrost, the fruit and vegetable place that has a great juice bar.

We get out of the car.

Squash and pumpkins are on the tables.

Jim goes inside and picks up corn, broccoli, spinach, and fruit. Being a vegetarian is something he takes very seriously. Mindy, however, loves meat, coffee, and junk food, all the stuff he hates. It makes our kitchen cupboards look very interesting.

After he's done shopping, we sit at the side of the building where the juice bar is set up.

"What would you like to order today?" Cathy, the woman behind the counter, asks.

"The creamsicle," I say. It's the one made of yogurt, orange juice, and maple syrup.

Jim asks for a glass of orange juice.

It's so much fun to watch the orange juice machine. Cathy throws whole oranges in and the machine slices and squeezes them in minutes.

"Food?" Cathy asks.

Jim orders the power breakfast, although it's late in the day. It's made with green and sweet apples, ground nuts, three kinds of berries, maple syrup, and orange juice. Mindy would have taken me for an ice cream sundae.

I order the avocado plate with chips and salsa.

As we eat, I sit and look around at the greenhouse and gardens by the stand.

"Woodstock in the fall is a great place, isn't it, Phoebe?" Jim smiles.

"I'm Rosie," I say, staring at him. "Not Phoebe."

He looks confused. "I didn't call you Phoebe, did I, Rosie?"

I nod, frowning.

"I'm sorry, Rosie." Jim looks upset. "I know who you are. I guess it's just that I felt so comfortable with you that it was like old times with Phoebe."

That doesn't please me.

He continues: "What I'm trying to say is that I feel like you're my daughter."

"Like Phoebe." I'm getting even less pleased.

He shakes his head. "Like my second daughter, Rosie."

That makes me feel better.

I guess I can forgive him for calling me Phoebe because he felt close to me. It's kind of like when kids in school call their teachers "Mommy" by mistake. I, of course, called my third-grade teacher "Mindy."

Jim says, "Look, Rosie. I'm having a wonderful time with you. Please don't let it be ruined because of my mistake."

He looks miserable.

Poor Jim. He tries so hard to have everything turn out well and it's just not going the way he'd like it.

I smile at him and shake his hand. "Pals."

"Pals." He grins.

Jim's had a lot of trouble being a father.

I'm going to try to make it easy for him to be my stepfather.

22

Study hall. . . . It's so boring.

One kid's reading a comic book behind his geometry text.

Another's playing tic-tac-toe with the kid next to him, on the back of the kid in front of him.

I'm doodling in my notebook, writing in JASON 'N' ROSIE. Then I write JASON CARSON. Then I think about what if we got married and took each other's names. All three of his names would end with SON. If I took his name, two out of three would end that way.

I doodle it out on a new sheet of paper:

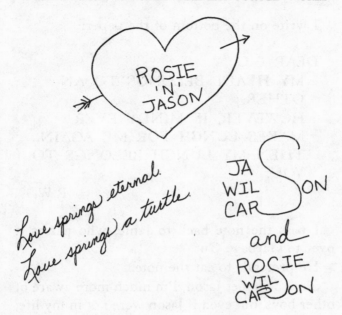

Someone taps me on the shoulder.

I check out the study hall teacher. He's busy reading the stock quotations in the newspaper.

Turning around, I take the note that is being passed to me by Janie Gams.

It's yet another marriage proposal from Garbage Gut.

DEAR ROSIE,
 WILL YOU MARRY ME?
 DID YOUR MOTHER PACK YOUR
 LUNCH FOR YOU TODAY?
                          G.G.

I write on the bottom of the paper:

DEAR G.G.,
  MY HEART BELONGS TO AN-
OTHER.
  HOWEVER, IF MINDY EVER
MAKES LUNCH FOR ME AGAIN,
THEN MY LUNCH BELONGS TO
YOU.
                                    R.W.

I pass the note back to Janie, who passes it
over to Garbage Gut.

He pretends to eat the note.

Since I've met Jason, I'm much more aware of
other boys, but even if Jason were not in my life,
I seriously doubt that Garbage Gut would be.

The intercom buzzes.

Everyone in the room jumps, afraid that it's
for them and they'll be in trouble.

That includes the study hall teacher, who's
only trying to hold on till retirement.

It's for me.

I'm being called to the front office.

I can't figure out what I did.

Even though I know I haven't done anything
wrong, I'm still nervous. In schools, you're
guilty until you're proven innocent.

Getting to the front office, I see Mindy standing there, waiting for me.

I hope that nothing terrible's happened to Jim or Phoebe or my father.

Running up to her, I say, "What's wrong?"

She's grinning from ear to ear. "Nothing. Read this."

She hands me a letter.

I take the envelope that she's handed me. I pull out the letter and read it.

Mindy's just sold her first book.

Life does go on.

Hooray for our team.

23

"My mother, the author." I raise my orange juice glass to toast Mindy as we sit on the porch of Deanie's Restaurant.

Mindy clinks her glass to mine. "Your mother, the fibber—who told the school that you had to leave because of an emergency doctor's appointment."

"I feel paroled." I keep grinning. "Oh, Mindy, I'm so proud of you."

The waitress comes up to take our order. She knows Mindy's a waitress, too, and she's really nice to us.

After she leaves, I say, "Can you quit your job now?"

Mindy shakes her head. "Honey, don't expect

too much. First of all, they said they'd buy it, but that I'd have to do revisions. Then it takes at least a year before it gets published, and then maybe some money will start coming in six months after that. I'll be getting some advance money, which will help pay bills and will put some money in your college fund, but we're definitely not going to be wealthy. . . . Maybe someday . . . but Rosie, don't expect it."

If I'm going to be a writer, I'd better be prepared to have another job too.

Taking a sip of my orange juice, I say, "I thought it would be like winning the lottery."

"No," Mindy says, "it doesn't work that way, but just think—you'll be able to go into a bookstore and buy *Frogs in My Locker* by Mindy Kovacs."

"Won't you give me a copy?"

"Not only give you a copy but dedicate it to you," Mindy tells me.

"Oh, Mom." I love her so much.

She puts her hand on my cheek. "You haven't called me Mom since you were five years old, came home from kindergarten, and announced that since it was just the two of us, we'd be pals and on a first-name basis."

We just look at each other for a few minutes, and then I say, "So tell me everything. What happened when you got the letter? . . . What did Jim say?"

She says, "I went out to our mailbox and there

it was. I was so scared that it would be another rejection letter. I opened it up right there . . . and then I jumped into my car and went over to Jim's studio."

"What did he say?" I ask again.

Since the waitress is bringing us our food, Mindy waits until she leaves and says, "He was excited, sort of. It's hard . . . I interrupted him in the middle of his painting. I've never gone over there while he's working."

"But you've gone over there with him sometimes at night."

Mindy blushes. "He's not painting then."

Now we're both blushing. "So was he pleased or not?"

She nods. "Yes. He was. He hugged me and we jumped up and down. Then we talked about what to do with the money. He said it was all mine. I said it was the family's money. He didn't say anything.

"I asked if he still considered us a family." Mindy looks very serious. "It was so hard to talk about. He said that he did, sort of, but he missed Phoebe and wanted her to be part of our family."

"Sort of!" I can't believe it. "How can he say that? And how can he be such a big down on the day that your book gets accepted? That sounds like something Phoebe would do."

Mindy takes my hand. "Rosie. I know this is all very complicated. Jim and Phoebe are alike in some ways. They're both very self-involved, but Jim is really trying to grow out of it."

"Why stay with him if he's like that?" I'm getting upset.

"Do you love Jim?" Mindy says.

"Yes. Most of the time." I nod. "Even when he sings 'We're Off to See the Gizard.' "

"I love him too," Mindy says. "Rosie, he's not perfect, but neither am I. We love each other, are able to laugh and have a good time. We can also talk to each other about problems. We try very hard to communicate. That's more than I can say about a lot of people. Nobody has a perfect relationship."

"I want to," I say, thinking of Jason.

Mindy shakes her head. "Honey, don't expect perfection. It'll only cause trouble. That's what happened with your father's and my marriage. We had unrealistic expectations about what marriage should be and weren't able to work at making the changes. Now after all those years I've finally met someone I want to be with and I'm working harder at it than I ever did. And so is Jim."

"Is he really working at it?"

"Yes, but Phoebe's leaving has really hurt him and there are moments when he wonders if he made the right choice or if we should have waited."

"I hate Phoebe." I stab at my lunch.

"Try not to." Mindy shakes her head. "Phoebe's having a difficult time right now. She's a person who really needs a structure, and the divorce and her parents' being with other people has really thrown her for a loop."

"Other kids don't act that way."

"Some do," Mindy continues. "And I don't think even when her parents were together that Phoebe was given a strong structure and taught the best way to act."

"You're being too nice. She's really tried to screw things up." I think of how she acted in Canada too.

Mindy nods. "True. There are days I want to wring her neck . . . and I'm really glad she's out of the house if she's going to try to break Jim and me up. But remember last year—she was very lovable, sweet, and fun."

"I remember. It makes me sad that she's not like that again." I can feel tears start even though I don't think I care anymore.

"It's a tough time for her," Mindy says.

"I don't want to stay home when she comes. Do you think I should?"

"Decide for yourself. There's no right or wrong," Mindy says.

I think about it. "I don't want to see her . . . and I don't want to talk about her anymore. Let's talk about the book."

Mindy smiles. "Honey, you've always been so helpful around the house so that I could write. And I appreciate your reading the book and giving me suggestions. So I want to buy something very special for you. Think about what you'd like. Don't ask for something for someone else. Pick a present for yourself. I want it to be very special so that when you are very old, you can look at it and say, 'We got that when Mindy sold her first book.' "

"You don't have to get me anything. I did those things because I wanted to."

"I'm not doing it because I have to. I'm doing it because I want to," Mindy tells me.

I think about it. "There's this fabulous silver mirror at Anne Smith Antiques that I always go in to visit."

"The one with the beautiful face carved on it?" Mindy and I like a lot of the same things.

"Is it too expensive?" I want to know.

Mindy shrugs. "It's definitely not cheap . . . but it's perfect. Let's go over there after lunch and ask Anne to put it away until my check comes in."

I'm so excited.

I love that mirror.

I'm so proud of Mindy.

I'm also very glad that she's brought me up the way she has.

24

The Little Nerdlet has an imaginary playmate, Berky.

This is a new development.

Mrs. Donner thinks it's because they've just brought home the Little Nerdlet II, actually a Nerdlette, Dawna.

Berky put peanut butter in the Venus flytrap. The plant closed up, wouldn't reopen, and died. He also wet the Little Nerdlet's bed and the Little Nerdlet's parents' bed.

The Little Nerdlet said he tried to stop Berky but couldn't.

Mrs. Donner hopes he'll grow out of it.

I'm not so sure. Donny said Berky was willing to sell Dawna to me.

The Little Nerdlet and I are playing on the swings at Andy Lee Field.

It's Sunday and there's a softball league game on the baseball field.

The Little Nerdlet takes Berky up the slide.

As I wait to catch him/them, I look at the guys playing ball. Some of them are kind of cute but none as cute as Jason.

The Little Nerdlet comes down the slide.

I catch him.

I forget to catch Berky though.

The Little Nerdlet picks up his friend and tells me to check for boo-boos.

It's a little embarrassing to dust off an imaginary playmate.

"Kiss the boo-boo," the Little Nerdlet orders me.

I refuse.

The Little Nerdlet cries.

I kiss the boo-boo.

"Hi, Rosie."

It's Phoebe. Dave is with her.

The Little Nerdlet puts his arms around her left leg and kisses her kneecap.

"I could be very jealous of this kid," Dave says.

I don't know what to say. Folding my arms across my chest, I just stand there.

"Can we talk?" Phoebe asks.

"About what?"

"Please," Phoebe says. "Dave will watch Donny."

"And Berky," the Little Nerdlet informs her.

"Berky?" Phoebe asks.

I put my arm around "Berky." "This is Donny's new friend."

Phoebe smiles at me and I smile back. It's the first time since our trip to Canada that anything nice has happened between us.

"Okay." I nod. "But Dave has to take Donny *and* Berky."

"Come on, guys. Let's go," Dave says.

Off they go. Dave is Donny's idol. He'll follow him anywhere.

I keep my arms folded across my chest and just stand here.

"You're not going to make it easy to talk, are you?" Phoebe says, quietly.

"Should I?" My voice is ice.

Phoebe looks like she's going to leave, but doesn't.

I stare at her.

"Yes," she says. "Maybe not easy but possible. I'm here to talk about what's happened—how I feel—how I miss you."

"How about how I feel? Does that count? Or are we only supposed to talk about you?" I continue to stare at her.

"Both of us should talk." She sighs. "Rosie, I don't want to beg for this talk."

"You're the one who walked out on the family," I tell her.

"And I'm the one who's trying to walk back in, and you won't even discuss it. You're the one who says you want a family . . . but you want one without any problems."

"That's not true." I defend myself.

"Yes, it is." She accuses me.

Maybe she's not totally wrong, but is it a crime because I want it that way?

She continues. "I want us to try to work things out as a family."

"All of a sudden we're a family again." I frown. "Things must be really terrible in New York."

Neither of us says anything.

I go over to the swings and sit down.

Phoebe stays where she is.

So now she wants to come home. Am I supposed to jump up and down and applaud? Have her come home and be the center of attention all the time by being a problem? What does she want from me? Sainthood?

Who cares?

I do. "Phoebe, come sit on the swings. Let's talk."

Phoebe sits down on the swing next to me and starts to cry.

I hate it when she cries.

"Rosie, everything's so messed up." She continues to cry. "I haven't been really happy for so long."

"You could have been happy if you'd stayed here," I tell her.

"No," she says. "It's been hard since even before my parents' divorce."

Mindy was right.

The tears are rolling down Phoebe's face. "I just got used to Dad and me in Woodstock and then he started to spend all that time with Mindy and I felt left out. And my mother married Duane and I felt like she didn't have much time for me. Then when we went to Canada, you met Jason and didn't have time for me."

"But you have Dave," I tell her. "And everyone does care about you and spend time with you."

"I guess I just need a lot." Phoebe wipes the tears off with her sleeve. "And I hate living with Duane. He really doesn't like me, and Mom's off at work a lot. It's so hard. Here I have people who really do care, but there's not much to do. In New York I love all the stuff to do, but I don't have the people."

"So you do know how Mindy and Jim feel about you."

Phoebe nods. "I do now."

I start to swing a little.

So does Phoebe.

"I miss Dave so much, and I miss you too." Phoebe looks at me.

We don't say anything for a while but try to work it out so that the swings go the same way and the same speed.

"Are you moving back?" I ask.

Phoebe says, "I talked to Dad and Mindy about it. They said it's okay with them if I'm willing to make changes and to get some counseling."

"Are you?"

She nods. "Yes. I hate being this miserable, and I think it'll help me. Mom asked me to stay until Christmas, at least, so that we can continue to try to work out our relationship. I said yes because I want things to be better with her too."

"And then you'll come back?" I want to know.

"Yes. If it's okay with you. I don't want us to have big problems anymore. And you wouldn't have to share a room this time. Mindy says that now that she's got some money she'll rent an office in town and I can move into her house office."

"She said she'd give up her office?" I'm amazed.

"She said she was doing it for you, not for me."

"Wow." I stop the swing. "Mindy's going to do that? If you come back, will you be nicer to Mindy? And work on our being a family?"

Phoebe stops her swing. "I'll really try."

I get off the swing and hold my arms out. "Welcome home."

We hug each other.

I'm beginning to realize that being a family doesn't mean that everything goes smoothly . . . and that maybe I shouldn't even expect it to. I also am beginning to see that there can be love even if there's not always like.

25

Christmas Eve in Woodstock. It's the most special time and place in the world.

This year's even more wonderful because Jason's here.

Standing on the village green, we're in the middle of a crowd singing carols and waiting for Santa Claus. Jason's got his arm around my waist and my head is on his shoulder.

We stopped at the Little Nerdlet's house before coming into town. We decided to exchange presents tonight. For Dawna, I bought this adorable baby flannel tuxedo from Camp Kinderland, a great store in town. She drooled all over it. I gave the Little Nerdlet the mouse earmuffs that I got in Canada. He said, "Oh, goody! Headphones!" and was very disappointed that they weren't attached to a radio. The Little Nerdlet said he would share it with Berky, since I forgot to get a present for him. The Donners gave me this pair of earrings I've been staring at for months from Sweetheart Gallery.

Everyone is waiting for Santa Claus.

The snow is coming down lightly.

Jason and I are huddled together for warmth and for happiness.

Garbage Gut comes up to us. He always comes to town on Christmas Eve because all the stores give out free food and drinks. "So this is the famous Jason who stole Rosie's heart."

I tell Garbage Gut that Vidakafka's giving out delicious homemade almond butter cookies. He rushes off, even though it's a store that sells beautiful lingerie. He has no shame. Nothing stops G.G. when it involves food. It's a good thing he's a growing boy and that he exercises or he'd be in trouble.

Mindy, Jim, Phoebe, and Dave join us. We link arms and sing "White Christmas."

I think of my father and his family in California. They wanted me to go out there for the holidays but I said no, that I wanted to be here. My father accused me of having no sense of family. I promised to go there over spring break.

"He's coming. He's coming," people in the crowd start to call out.

I look up at Jason and smile.

We kiss.

"He's here."

We stop kissing to see Santa Claus arrive on a giant float shaped like a plane, with a sign on it, "The Spirit of Woodstock."

Each year he arrives a different way. It's the best tradition.

After getting off the float, he stands in the middle of the village green and starts handing out stockings filled with candy, fruit, and little toys.

The snow is coming down heavier. Some of the older kids are throwing snowballs at each other.

There's a long line of little kids waiting for Santa. Garbage Gut is in the middle, bending at his knees so that he looks shorter.

People on the village green are wishing each other a happy holiday. Others are going into the stores for last-minute shopping and visiting with the people who have to work on Christmas Eve.

Phoebe comes over smiling and says, "Let's go home and trim the tree."

I nod and smile back.

Jim is tap dancing in the snow to the tune of "Frosty the Snowman," which is being sung by Mindy and Dave.

Jason kisses me on the forehead. "I love Woodstock."

"I knew you would." I put my right hand in his and take Phoebe's hand with my left.

It's not a dog-eat-dog world.
It's not even an aardvark-eat-turtle world.
It's a world where families and friendships change and grow.
It sure takes a lot of work, but it's worth it.

About the Author

PAULA DANZIGER was born in Washington, D.C., because, her parents said, "that way no state could disown her." A short while later the family moved to New Jersey, where they remained except for a brief time spent on a farm in Holidaysburg, Pennsylvania.

Now that Paula Danziger is grown-up, she divides her time between New York City, where she has never mugged anyone, and Woodstock, where she eats granola, plays video games, and puts stickers on everything.

A